Praise for
Clear Winter Nights

"Trevin Wax's *Clear Winter Nights* is an engaging story about something fresh and vital—the old kind of Christian, transformed by Christ, doing battle with sin, relying on Jesus day after day. The book raises honest questions and offers honest answers based on what's rock solid, not on our culture's ever-shifting worldview. I enjoyed the moving relationship between a young man and an old one, with history, heritage, mentoring, and friendship. I found *Clear Winter Nights* to be warm, compelling, and thought provoking."

> —RANDY ALCORN, author of *Heaven, Deception,*
> and *If God Is Good*

"The best novels leave you wanting more. As I read *Clear Winter Nights,* I wanted to join the characters' conversations and felt the pain of separation from them when I finished. Trevin Wax has given us the gift of a compelling story about family, doubt, faith, and the biggest questions of life."

> —COLLIN HANSEN, editorial director for The Gospel
> Coalition and co-author of *A God-Sized Vision:*
> *Revival Stories That Stretch and Stir*

"Trevin Wax takes you on an honest intellectual and emotional journey as he explores the exclusive claims of Christ that everyone has struggled with at some time or another. His characters draw the reader into the conversation and leave you feeling satisfied about where they end up, bringing in a whole new dynamic to how we typically approach theological study."

> —MATT CARTER, co-author of *The Real Win*

"'Tell all the truth, but tell it slant,' said Emily Dickinson. This book does exactly that. This book goes to the guts of the gospel, and it shares the good news story straight by telling it slant. Thank you, Trevin Wax, for putting your imagination as well as your theology in service to Christ."

> —TIMOTHY GEORGE, dean of Beeson Divinity School
> at Samford University and general editor of the
> Reformation Commentary on Scripture

"Chris is struggling with his faith in God, his relationships are falling apart, and he doesn't know where to turn. He doesn't have to go far to find a faithful friend in his grandfather. Trevin Wax's *Clear Winter Nights* tackles faith, doubt, theology, the person of Christ, evangelism, and our struggle with sin. Clear and insightful; the pages pour out God's amazing grace to sinners and His unfailing love to those who've wandered away. A perfect book for anyone with questions about faith in the one true God."

> —TRILLIA NEWBELL, author and writer, and editor
> of *Women of God Magazine*

CLEAR WINTER NIGHTS

CLEAR

A journey into truth, doubt,

WINTER

and what comes after

NIGHTS

TREVIN WAX

MULTNOMAH
BOOKS

CLEAR WINTER NIGHTS
PUBLISHED BY MULTNOMAH BOOKS
12265 Oracle Boulevard, Suite 200
Colorado Springs, Colorado 80921

All Scripture quotations, unless otherwise noted, are taken from the King James Version. Scripture quotations marked (ESV) are taken from The Holy Bible, English Standard Version, copyright © 2001 by Crossway Bibles, a division of Good News Publishers. Used by permission. All rights reserved.

The characters and events in this book are fictional, and any resemblance to actual persons or events is coincidental.

Hardcover ISBN: 978-1-60142-494-5
eBook ISBN: 978-1-60142-495-2

Cover design by Mark D. Ford

Published in the United States by WaterBrook Multnomah, an imprint of the Crown Publishing Group, a division of Random House Inc., New York.

MULTNOMAH and its mountain colophon are registered trademarks of Random House Inc.

Library of Congress Cataloging-in-Publication Data
Wax, Trevin, 1981–
    Clear winter nights : a journey into truth, doubt, and what comes after / Trevin Wax.—
First edition.
        pages cm
    ISBN 978-1-60142-494-5 (hardback)—ISBN 978-1-60142-495-2 (ebook)
  1. Male college students—Fiction. 2. Adult children of divorced parents—Fiction.
3. Grandparents—Fiction. 4. Faith—Fiction. 5. Forgiveness—Fiction. 6. Knoxville
(Tenn.)—Fiction. 7. Psychological fiction. I. Title.
    PS3623.A892C54 2013
    813'.6—dc23

                                                            2013017699

Printed in the United States of America
2013—First Edition

10 9 8 7 6 5 4 3 2 1

SPECIAL SALES
Most WaterBrook Multnomah books are available at special quantity discounts when purchased in bulk by corporations, organizations, and special-interest groups. Custom imprinting or excerpting can also be done to fit special needs. For information, please e-mail SpecialMarkets@WaterBrookMultnomah.com or call 1-800-603-7051.

For William Browder Wyatt,
Nevin Wax, and Bill Alexander

Saturday, October 7, Knoxville, Tennessee

C an we leave now? I don't want to be late," Ashley said, tugging at Chris's arm and drawing him out of his thoughts. It was late afternoon, and she had stopped by the apartment her fiancé shared with a couple of other college students in the run-down Fort Sanders neighborhood in Knoxville. The two were about to head to a meeting for a new church start-up they were involved in.

Ashley always sought to make a good impression. That's one reason Chris liked her. Self-aware without being self-absorbed. She was cute too. Small, with shoulder-length strawberry-blond hair.

"I don't feel like going," Chris said, meeting her smile with a furrowed brow and hoping she could sense his irritation. The sunlight coming in at a low angle through the window touched his wavy dark hair.

Ashley pressed on. "I told Luke and Cami we'd be there."

"Is it okay with you if we just walk?"

"I guess," she said. Her sigh said it wasn't.

Chris grabbed a jacket, and the two turned toward the door. As they left, Chris was wondering, *Should I go ahead and say it to her today? Do I really want to?* He sighed and turned the key in the lock.

OCTOBER IN EAST TENNESSEE. The trees were surrendering their leaves, and the sidewalk and street edges were hiding under a blanket of harvest colors. One more hour of daylight would give them enough time for a walk and a talk.

Chris was a gentleman. He made sure he walked on the outside, next to the street, and that his wiry frame was shielding Ashley's eyes from the slanting sunlight. He escorted her, arm in arm, with an air of old-fashioned sophistication. They passed one large old house after another, most of them long since converted to student housing for the University of Tennessee.

Ashley asked him, "Are you having second thoughts about helping start the church?"

Chris didn't answer. Didn't Ashley realize this conversation could go south? Maybe she did. Maybe that's what she wanted. If she insisted, he would oblige.

"I… Yeah, I'm having second thoughts about…about a lot of things," he said.

Chris saw concern on Ashley's face. But she covered it with an uneasy smile and leaned in closer to his side as they walked.

Just a few months earlier, Chris had his life mapped out. He'd finally given Ashley a ring, and the two were planning to get married next spring. He was supposed to graduate from college in the summer, help a friend start a business, and take on a leadership role in the new church start-up.

But one by one, all his plans had fallen through. An unexpected class requirement postponed his graduation until December. His friend decided to start his business somewhere else. When it came to church, Chris was waffling on more than just being a part of the church-planting team. And the longer he was with Ashley, the more he wondered if his ring was really a fit for her finger.

"I'm here for you, no matter what," Ashley said. She stroked the inside of his palm. "Are you still having doubts?"

"Doubts?" Chris tried to act surprised.

"You know, doubts about the new church, about what you believe."

Doubt sounded like a bad word the way Ashley used it. "It's not really doubting," he said. "It's more like…questioning." That was better. But Chris knew he wasn't fooling her.

"Okay." Ashley played along. "Questions, then. Has Dr. Coleman gotten under your skin lately?"

An image of his religion professor's tall figure and unremitting gaze entered Chris's mind. "No more than usual," he said. "Some, I guess. He's definitely got me thinking."

"He does that to lots of his students. I had a hard time for a while too. But in the end, I think I came out stronger for it."

"Yeah, well, we're different," he said. He knew she was trying to help, but it wasn't working.

"Have you told Luke about any of this?"

"He's got enough on his plate."

"He wouldn't mind."

"He's trying to start a church. Last thing he needs is for one of us to tell him we're not bought in one hundred percent."

"Well," Ashley said, "if he sees you like this, he's going to think you're not bought into his vision, anyway. He might think he's done something to upset you. That it's because of him."

"It's not."

"But he doesn't know that. He doesn't know the doubts you have."

"Questions."

"Right. Questions. He's always saying the church needs to be a place for people to be real. To doubt. To question."

"I don't think Luke is ready for his leaders to be this real."

Both were quiet for a few moments. Then Ashley said, "Have you talked to your grandfather?"

At the mention of his grandfather, Chris felt a wave of joy crash into a shore of guilt. Gilbert Walker was a retired pastor who lived in the charming old town of Lewisville, about ninety miles west of Knoxville. At eighty years of age, Chris's grandfather seemed to be in good health, sharp in mind and strong in body. He and Chris couldn't get together without losing themselves in interesting conversation, sometimes even argument. But the house was out of the way, nestled in the hill country, and Chris hadn't visited as often as he thought he should—only for lack of time, not for lack of love.

"It's too soon," he said. "Grandma's only been gone a month."

"Maybe you're right," Ashley said. "But I bet he'd enjoy the company."

Chris nodded. Ashley was always thinking of others and seemed to know instinctively when people's gifts and personalities would complement one another. Just bring the right person to the right place at the right time for the right meeting, and everyone would be stronger.

As they walked past the old brick Christ Chapel, Chris thought again of their church-planting team. "So you think I should talk to Luke?"

Ashley's response came so quickly it caught Chris off guard. "For sure. That's what he's there for. You're not supposed to walk this road alone. I don't know what I would've done without some older, wiser people around me." Then she added, "I know what you're going through."

Chris felt his temperature rise. Ashley's attempts at empathy were working against her. He started to think of all the things that made his situation so much more difficult than hers had been. He remembered when she had gone through her "dark night of the soul." Aptly named, because it seemed as though it lasted only one night. Chris, on the other hand, had been wrestling for months, and the nights were only getting darker. Is there a dark year of the soul?

"You're not me," he said.

"I never said that," Ashley said, slower and quieter. "But no matter who you are, you need others. You can't hold on to a childlike faith if you don't grab hold of a grownup every now and then."

"There's a difference between a childlike faith and a childish faith," Chris said.

"Chris Walker—" She bit her lip and turned away from him, doing her trademark eye roll used to keep from crying.

"No, Ashley. Seriously."

"So I have a childish faith?"

"I didn't say that." Chris groaned. "Come on, Ashley, you know I admire the way you've thought through things. I think it's great you've gotten stronger through everything. Last thing I want is for you to turn into me."

He grinned. She returned the smile, noticeably halfhearted.

Chris continued, "It's just…you know what Luke's been saying. How this church is going to require commitment, more than any other church we've been a part of before."

"You said that's a good thing."

"Yeah. It is. I think. But it's a little scary too. Luke even wants us to sign a covenant that says what we believe."

"Does that bother you?"

"No. I think it's awesome."

"Then what's the problem?" Ashley's tone betrayed her exasperation.

"I don't know," Chris confessed. "I just want to be sure that I really believe all this stuff before I commit. I don't want to be the guy who's telling other people to get right with God, to come to church, to love Jesus and all that, when I'm not one hundred percent sure of everything I'm saying. You know, about God...truth...morality...and Jesus...the Bible."

"You're doubting all those things?"

"Not completely." Chris's response wasn't reassuring, even to himself. "I guess I just don't know how everything fits together anymore. Not just what is true but why it's true. Why it matters. And I want to get this right. I don't want to be a hypocrite."

"I like that about you," Ashley said. "But isn't there a point where you need to open up and ask for help when you've got so many questions?" She delivered the question sweetly, but there was no way for Chris to keep from feeling judged.

"God wouldn't give us minds if He didn't expect us to use them."

She cringed at his jab. "Questions are supposed to lead to answers, Chris."

Before Chris could say something he might have regretted, his telephone buzzed. It was a text from Luke. "Hey, man, are you and Ashley good? The gang's all here. Just checking in before we get going."

He shot a text back: "Not going to make it tonight. Talk soon."

A COUPLE OF MINUTES PASSED in silence as they continued to walk together. Chris could hear a train rumbling in the distance. The sun slipped behind one of the mountain peaks and left him and Ashley in twilight. The chill in the air caused him to pull the hood of his jacket over his head, and it reminded him of the first time they met.

They'd been at a bonfire for their campus Christian fellowship, and the reflection of the flames had flickered in her eyes. She was trying to roast a hot dog but found the fire too hot to let her get close enough. Half the hot dog was blackened, and the other half felt as if it were still refrigerated. Chris offered to roast another one for her. He singed the hair off his knuckles trying to get it done just right, but once he was finished, she had a perfectly roasted hot dog. And he had won the right to a chat with her. It was to be the first of many. But lately their talks had gotten increasingly difficult.

"This is about your dad, isn't it?"

She really did it. She dropped the dad bomb.

Chris felt a tightness grip his chest and started to quiver. "No," he said. Firmly. As if he could shut down that conversation with will-power alone. "Maybe," he added weakly. He shrugged and sighed. "I don't know."

September 12. Chris would never forget the date he found out everything. That was the date of Grandma Frances's funeral, and he was in Lewisville with his mom, his grandfather, and a bunch of other relatives. He kept looking for his father to show up, but Christopher Walker Sr. never appeared.

Chris had been puzzled. After the divorce nine years ago, his father and mother never got together anymore. Come to think of it, he'd never seen his father with any other relatives, though he knew his father would get in touch with his grandfather occasionally. But this was his own mother's funeral—where was he?

After the service, Chris mentioned his disappointment over his father's absence to his favorite cousin, Dave.

"Come on, you're surprised?" said Dave. "No offense, but that jerk can't be trusted for anything."

Chris couldn't believe what he was hearing. Although he hadn't seen his father much since the divorce, he'd always looked up to him as a saint, as a role model, even from a distance. He'd viewed him as a long-suffering husband who'd been forced to leave the family and make a new life for himself.

But at the funeral, all of Chris's illusions had been torn down as Dave proceeded to spill the salacious details of the events that had led to his parents' divorce. The specificity of Dave's knowledge of these events, and the confidence in his tone, left little doubt that Dave was telling the truth. More than that, it all fit. The pieces of information he had picked up over the years without understanding them, the history his parents and grandparents had left unspoken, and the circumstances he had always blamed on his mother—everything became clear.

He'd had everything backward. His father was the hypocritical lowlife, and his mother was the honorable one who'd refused to divulge the details out of respect for Chris's view of his dad. Respect his dad never deserved.

Ashley brought him back to the present. "It *is* about your dad."

She was right. Dr. Coleman bothered Chris, but it was his father's deception and hypocrisy that had forced Chris into a sea of doubt. And here he was now, kicking and struggling toward the surface, drowning in his questions. If his father could fake his faith so well all those years, maybe the faith itself was false.

Ashley continued. "He made decisions that affected you and your mom. Those were his decisions."

"Yeah, but I have to live with them," Chris said. "I can't believe how stupid I was. All those years I thought of him as the righteous one."

"You've got to forgive him and move on," Ashley said matter-of-factly.

Nothing enraged Chris more than Ashley's quick counsel to forgive and forget. As if his relationship with his dad were something he had to get over so he and Ashley could begin their picture-perfect life together.

Neither said anything for a few minutes. They walked on.

Chris finally broke the silence, speaking quietly and controlling his voice. "I don't know if this is going to work." He didn't have to elaborate.

She stopped walking, seemed to try to respond, but couldn't.

He went on, "M-maybe if we took a breather, a little time—"

Ashley pulled her hand from his. She was fighting back tears, choking back words.

"I don't mean that we break up," Chris said, backtracking. But the damage had been done. He'd cast the idea out there, and there was no reeling it back in.

"It's all me, Ashley. I just…I need to get some clarity on some things."

"Oh, Chris," Ashley said, backing away from him and wiping away her tears. She ran off in the direction of her own apartment.

CHRIS STOOD IN PLACE AWHILE, then plodded to "the strip" and found a bar, quiet at this early hour. He sank into a seat in the front where he could watch people going by outside, then ordered a burger and a beer.

Had he really done it? Broken his engagement? Given up Ashley forever? The Ashley he'd had so many wonderful dates with and spent so many hours spilling out his heart to? The Ashley he'd pictured himself spending the rest of his life with?

For a moment, he thought of jumping up from the table to chase after her, begging her to forget what he'd said.

But then he stopped himself. No, there was a real problem here. He had to figure out what he believed...or didn't believe. Ashley had a rock-solid faith in God and a firm understanding of who she was and who she wanted to be. But Chris was in quicksand. And as he sank, he told himself, he had no business marrying her.

Even though the burger looked delicious, Chris somehow couldn't take more than a single bite. But the beer was going down easily. He was just about to order something stronger to drink when his phone's ringtone activated. It was his mom. He groaned, not in the mood to talk, but answered anyway.

"Hey," he said.

His mother spoke rapidly. "Chris, I'm on my way to the hospital in Crossville. They've taken your grandpa there in an ambulance. They think he's had a stroke."

Chris was stunned. Just a month before, they'd buried his grandmother after her stroke. Was he about to lose his grandpa too, and in the same way?

"What happened?"

"Ruth went over there today as usual, and she found him on the floor. She said his speech was slurred and he couldn't move his left side. It's bad."

"I'm coming too. See you there." He pressed a button to end the call.

He slapped a handful of bills on the table and was gone.

Saturday, December 30, Lewisville, Tennessee

hris stepped out of the car, taking care to steady himself as he moved from the snow-covered driveway to the icy sidewalk. With one hand holding his duffel bag and his other hand held out for balance, he put one foot in front of the other, hoping he wouldn't slip.

It was not long after noon, but the sky was gray and dark. Above him were the branches of a majestic oak tree, encased in ice and ready to snap off and fall. The front porch wasn't far ahead. So he combined speed with caution, skating a few feet down the sidewalk and then hopping up onto the porch of the old house.

His grandfather's house was the one place where he knew he'd find stability even if the whole world were crumbling around him. Like the other houses spaced widely on this tree-lined street, it was built in the 1920s. The porch's wooden planks were still sturdy despite the chorus of creaking they gave up when he walked on them. To his right, in the corner of the L-shaped porch that wrapped around half the house, a porch swing slowly rocked in the wind.

He lifted his hand to rap on the door, when to his surprise, it swung open before he could touch it.

There stood his grandfather—tall, broad shouldered, with a head of white hair and a face full of wrinkles that showed up where years of smiling had left their mark. He looked tired, and his back was slightly hunched, seeming to carry the accumulated weight of his years. He was leaning on his cane and favoring his left leg. Even so, there was a youthful gleam in his eyes. He sported a pair of glasses that looked remarkably in vogue—not because they were new but because he had worn them so long they'd come back into style.

He beckoned Chris in with that familiar baritone voice of his. "You made it in! I was beginning to worry."

"Yeah, Gramps, I made it. Had a hard time getting up this morning." Chris didn't explain why. He was certain his grandfather wouldn't care to hear about his activities the night before. "I didn't leave on time. The ice slowed me down."

"I'm just glad you're here."

More than two months had passed since the stroke. Chris's grandpa looked much better than he had when Chris had last seen him in the hospital in nearby Crossville. The physical therapy must have been working.

Chris stooped down to take off his shoes. They were caked in slush and mud.

"I told your mom I'd be fine this weekend," his grandfather said. "But she and Ruth insisted on having someone stay with me."

"I'm glad to be here, Gramps," Chris said, smiling. "You're looking good."

Chris looked around the front room. Nothing had changed in here for years. There, as usual, were the antique roll-top desk, the crowded bookshelves, the vast stone fireplace with the ticking clock on the mantel, Gil's worn leather recliner beside its lamp table, the faded couch in front of the picture window, and his grandmother's old upright piano.

Chris smiled at his grandfather again. "I'm upstairs, I guess."

"Of course," his grandpa said. He bent down to pick up Chris's bag.

"No, no, I've got it!" Chris wondered how his grandfather would have the balance to carry it. *He may be old, but he's persistent.*

Chris walked through the front room, then started up the narrow staircase. Behind him, he heard his grandfather say, "When you're done settling in, come on down and we'll have some lunch."

UPSTAIRS WERE THREE SMALL BEDROOMS and one bathroom. The ceilings were low and the hallway narrow. The flowered wallpaper made everything feel either cozy or cramped, depending on your taste. The thermostat was set too high, but Chris was just glad to be out of the cold. "Any room okay?" he shouted downstairs to his grandfather, who had shuffled to the foot of the staircase.

"Whatever you like."

Chris passed the first room without even looking in. It had belonged to his father. This was the room he had always stayed in when he was younger and visiting his grandparents. But now he had no intention of going in there.

At the end of the hall, he knew, was Aunt Ruth's old room. Definitely too feminine.

So the room across the hall was all that was left. It had always been a guest room. It had a big window overlooking the yard, with a window seat. The bed was covered with a bedspread that didn't match anything else and was flanked by an antiquated nightstand.

Chris unzipped his coat and draped it over a frail-looking rocking chair in the corner. He dropped his duffel bag on the floor and then flopped himself onto the bed, allowing the weight of the travel to catch up with him.

As long as his attention had been focused on surviving the car ride, his adrenalin had been flowing. He'd forgotten how tired he was. The hangover he'd woken up with that morning was almost gone, but in its place was an aching weariness that stole his remaining energy. Once he was in bed, the drowsiness took over. He would just rest his eyes.

As he lay in bed, an image of Ashley swam into his mind's eye. He remembered his phone call with her on Christmas afternoon. He'd wanted to call her—the first time since their disastrous conversation while out walking—just to reestablish a friendly, or at least polite, relationship with her. But as he spoke with her on the phone, he'd found himself remembering how much he used to enjoy spending time with her.

"I can call you again, can't I?" he'd asked at the end of the call.

He couldn't get her answer out of his mind. "Of course," she'd said. "But if you are trying to get back together, you'd better figure out what you want pretty soon. I expect you to be up-front with me, Chris Walker."

Maybe being here will help me sort things out, he thought.

His thoughts began to drift. He had just finished thinking, *I'd better get up and go down for lunch,* when he fell asleep.

WHEN CHRIS WOKE UP, it was turning dark outside. Dazed and disoriented, he thought he might be dreaming. He hadn't shut the curtains before lying down, and the tall oak trees outside waving in the breeze cast ominous shadows on the wall.

He rubbed his eyes and bolted out of bed, embarrassed at his lack of manners. *How did I fall asleep?* He looked at the clock now, and it said 6:03. *This can't be!* And then he realized the clock must be an hour ahead, never adjusted back after daylight saving time. So it was 5:03 p.m.

He headed downstairs, head still spinning, and called out, "Gramps?"

"I'm in here!" a deep voice rumbled from the living room.

Chris stumbled down the stairs and shielded his eyes from the light coming from the front room.

"Here he is!" Grandpa said, pride written all over his beaming face.

Once Chris's eyes adjusted to the light, he saw Grandpa sitting in his recliner near the fire. Across from his grandfather, sitting on the couch by the window, was a man of about sixty with a shiny head and a full beard.

"Chris, I don't think you've ever met Ronald Thurmond."

The two greeted each other and shook hands.

Ronald motioned for Chris to take a seat. There was enough room on the couch, but Chris felt odd about sitting next to the guest. So he pulled out the bench next to Grandma's piano and sat down on it saddle-style.

Chris stifled a yawn. "Sorry I slept."

"No need to apologize," Grandpa said. "I've been having a nice visit with my old friend here. Ron runs a law office downtown. In his spare time he helps direct the choir at my church." Even though he'd been retired for ten years, he still talked about Third Baptist Church as being his.

"How's the church doing?" Chris asked.

"Not badly," said Ron. "Gil here left things in good condition for the rest of us."

"Good condition?" His grandfather shook his head. "When the

church blew through two pastors after me? I've never been so disappointed in all my life. Personality conflicts, leadership struggles, unrealistic expectations. Why, the Methodists in town started saying, 'What's with them Baptists that they can't hold on to a good preacher?'"

"All in the past now," Ron said.

"Thank the Lord," Gil said.

"Your grandfather's something of a legend around town," Ron said, turning to Chris.

"Ah, come on now," Gil said.

"No, really! There isn't a week that goes by that someone doesn't ask me, 'What would Pastor Gil say?'"

"They oughta know by now what I'd say: 'Go see what God says.'" Gil put his hand on the worn black Bible sitting on top of the coffee table next to his recliner. "I don't understand why anyone cares what old Gil has to say. All I do is point people to what's in here. That's a lot more reliable than offering my measly old opinion." Gil chuckled.

Chris liked the thought of his granddad being the wise old sage of Lewisville, but he immediately sensed the spiritual distance between them. Yep, the old faithful pastor with his scoundrel of a son and doubting-Thomas grandson. If the people in town knew the family dynamics, it didn't stop them from revering Gil.

"Your grandfather is a reader," Ron said. He turned back to Gil. "I tell you, being an avid reader—that's what's kept your mind so sharp."

"Thanks, Ron...I think," Gil said. "I wonder if I ought to be offended."

"What do you mean?"

"That's a compliment with a put-down." Gil chuckled. "You compliment my sharp mind as if you're surprised. So there you go, reminding me of my age. You think my mind ought to be gone by now!"

"See what I mean? Sharp mind." Ron turned toward Chris and grinned. "You can hardly have a conversation with this guy! Really, Gil, maybe we take ourselves too seriously. We ought to have something other than a deep conversation every now and then."

"Au contraire," Gil said. The French words came out with a southern accent. "Deep conversations are the only ones worth having. The world is so full of meaningless drivel there's no need to add to it."

"Not to most people. What's the saying again? 'Politics and religion are not for polite company.'"

"Nonsense!" Gil was grumbling now. "If you ban politics and religion from polite conversation, you might as well go on and warn people they're going to be bored stiff."

"Do you have something against politeness?" Ron was needling Gil, and Chris was getting a kick out of watching the two interact.

"Of course not. I just worry that nowadays freedom *of* speech means freedom *from* speech. Like the freedom to talk about everything means we don't talk about anything…of substance, that is. Don't talk about death. Too morbid. Don't talk about sex. Too indelicate. Don't talk about politics. Too controversial. Don't talk about religion. Too off-putting. If you ask me, 'polite conversation' is a good way to shut down interesting conversation altogether."

"Exactly why I like coming over here," Ron said. "You've never been one to chat about the weather."

CHRIS SMILED AT THE TWO of them going on about ideas. During the pause that ensued, he thought of Dr. Coleman. He decided to insert something into the conversation.

"I agree. The best conversations are about significant things. There's not enough thinking going on in our day."

The older heads in the room turned toward Chris, decked out in his wrinkled T-shirt and jeans as he straddled the piano bench. The odd expressions on their faces reminded Chris of the vast difference in his age.

"O-of course, n-not everything can be deep," he stammered. "We ought to be balanced."

"Balance is overrated," Gil said. Chris realized his grandpa was going to act like Chris had been a part of the conversation from the beginning, which meant he wouldn't go easy on him. Even so, he was surprised to hear his grandpa contradict the first contribution he'd made to the conversation.

"So balance is a problem?" Ron said.

"Not a problem. Just overrated. I, for one, think you ought to be more focused on passion than balance. If all your passion and energy goes toward being balanced, you never run fast enough to make it past the finish line. But I say, if you just run, just pursue something—anything—balance will take care of itself."

"You're changing the subject, Gil. No one here is talking about running. We're talking about being balanced in conversation topics. You must admit the boy has a point."

Chris couldn't tell whether Ron's remark was a put-down or an affirmation. He was on record agreeing with Chris but was also calling him a boy.

"And what was his point again?" Gil asked. Chris was wondering himself.

Ron answered for him. "When it comes to discussion topics and matters of theology, one ought to be balanced. Lots of bad things have happened in the name of passion."

"Lots of good things haven't happened in the name of balance," Gil said. "Tell a guy who's in love he ought to be more levelheaded and balanced. Tell that to someone who feels deep down in his bones he's going to change the world. Seek ye first the kingdom, not balance."

THE ROOM WAS QUIET all of a sudden. At the first mention of level-headedness and love, Chris thought about his disintegrating relationship with Ashley. He decided to change the mood. "I'm hungry."

Gil smiled. "I bet you are. I've got some food ready for us in the kitchen, and Ron just stocked the pantry for us. We ought to last for a few days, anyway." Gil moved forward in his chair and straightened himself, ready to stand up. He tilted his head toward his friend. "You're welcome to join us, Ron."

Ron pushed up his sleeve, rotated the watch on his arm, and then held his arm far from his eyes so he could see the time. "No, Gil. I believe I've already stayed longer than I should have. Wanda's upset that I even ventured out tonight, what with the ice and all." He gathered his energy, slapped both hands on his knees, and stood up. He grabbed the overcoat he'd draped over the corner of the couch and extended his hand to Chris. "Delighted to meet you."

"Thanks for coming," Chris said.

"Will we be seeing you two at church tomorrow?" Ron asked.

Gil's face darkened at the thought of church. "With this ice, I guess I'd better not. I'm supposed to be especially careful about not falling."

"Everyone will understand," his guest reassured him.

"Thanks for coming by, Ron," Gil said. He hobbled slowly toward the kitchen, obviously trusting Chris to see Ron off.

Once Gil was past the staircase and out of earshot, Ron whispered to Chris. "He's doing much better than he was. Physically, that is. But it bothers him that he's not fully recovered yet. And to tell you the truth, he's not used to being in this big house all alone either. I'm glad you volunteered to come."

With that, he pressed a wrinkled business card into the palm of Chris's hand. "Call me if you need anything." Then he turned and disappeared through the front door.

"Still hungry?" Gil called from the kitchen.

"Coming."

While Chris was seeing off Ron, Gil was trying to get things ready for supper. He propped up his cane next to the table and grabbed hold of the countertop. He hesitated, not wanting to display his clumsiness in front of Chris, but he was determined to fend for himself.

Chris appeared in the doorway. "What's for dinner?" he asked.

"I know we've got some sandwich meat," Gil said. "But this weather's got me craving something hot." He pointed to the drawer under the oven. "Get a pot out of there, will you?"

Chris pulled out a pot and put it on the stove. He took the cans from Gil, opened a drawer, and fumbled around until he found the can opener. Then he dumped the soup contents into the pot, added some water, and turned the stove on.

Gil made his way to the table. "I'm always glad when Ron comes by," he said, more to himself than to Chris.

"How many visitors do you get a week, Gramps?"

"Well, your aunt comes around every day. There's a nurse from church who's helping me do some therapy. Some friends drop by with groceries. And Ron's been coming over about once a week."

"Do you wish you could get out more?" Chris asked.

He quickly turned his attention back to the stove, but Gil noticed that his ears were red. Probably embarrassed from asking a question with an answer so obvious. Gil smiled, his heart swelling with pride. Looking at Chris, he saw a younger version of himself—particularly in his propensity to speak before thinking!

"Sure, I do," he said. "But I'm learning some things by being stuck at home."

"Like what?"

"I used to think you had to go somewhere and see something grand if you wanted to experience life. Not anymore. Most fascinating things you see are what come across your path on an ordinary day. I guess sometimes you have to stand still to really see."

"Yeah?"

"I may be a little more limited than I would like, but I'm finding if you put your limitations to good use, they're like the frame around a portrait. They enhance everything around you. The sunrise and sunset are always different. The colors of the leaves will take your breath away. And they never fall the same way. So one day the back-yard is full of leaves; the next, they're matted down with rain; the next, they've been raked into piles and the neighbor's kid is splashing around in them as if they're a swimming pool."

Chris chuckled and nodded his head. Gil wondered if he knew he'd been thinking about the way Chris used to play out there.

"Yes sir, everything is changing. And sometimes the only way to really take in something, to understand its joy, is to be there—be present. Not running from one place to the next. Just being there. Rooted."

Chris turned from the stove to face his grandfather. "I think it's great you've got that perspective," he said.

Gil shrugged. "Don't get me wrong. I miss being as active as I used to be. When they took away the car, I felt like I had an arm or a leg chopped off." There was a tinge of resentment in his voice.

"But you were having a hard time driving, Gramps," Chris said. "Mom and Aunt Ruth were just trying to help."

"Oh, I know," Gil said. "They were right. But it still wasn't easy."

"You still get around here okay," Chris said. "And your recovery is going good. Who says you'll never drive again?"

Gil nodded his head, but he didn't feel any better. *Easy for you to say. You've got your whole life ahead of you.* He sensed a little root of bitterness digging down into his heart. He plucked it out before saying anything more. *Your very existence is only because of grace,* he told himself. *To be is to be graced.* Within a few seconds, the resentment was gone and his joy was back.

"Why don't you use the walker?" Chris asked. He nodded toward the corner where a state-of-the-art walker sat, complete with chair, brakes, wheels, and locks.

"Too fancy," Gil said. "The cane has more dignity. It may not be as flashy, but it does the trick."

While the soup was heating up, Chris reached over to the pantry and pulled out a box of crackers. Then he opened the refrigerator and found some slices of American cheese. Gil saw him glance at the sell-by date. "Don't worry. They're fresh," he said.

"You don't miss a thing, do you?" Chris said.

"Not much." Gil smiled. A pain shot through his leg all the way up to his hip. He groaned softly and shifted in his seat, trying to get comfortable.

"Your mom told me you have to be back at work on Tuesday. Still a manager at that trucking company, right?"

"Yep. It's not what I want to do forever, but it will pay some bills. I was going to help a friend get an online business going, but he went ahead by himself."

"By the way, congratulations on finishing college! I'm sorry I couldn't make it to the commencement."

"Oh, I understand."

"How's Ashley?" he asked next.

A pained look came over Chris's face. "That's over," he said shortly.

Gil nodded. "Still?"

"I'm guessing Mom already told you," said Chris.

"She did. That's why I wanted to ask you about it. I'm surprised you haven't changed your mind. You and Ashley seemed so happy with each other. I'm sorry."

Gil watched how Chris finished preparing the cheese and crackers. *His expression is older than his age,* he thought. *He looks twenty-two, all right, but there's a weariness in his face.*

"It never seemed you felt one way or the other about her," Chris said.

"Oh, I liked her. Sweet girl."

"Yeah, she is." Chris's voice betrayed a sense of regret. He put the cheese and crackers on the table and then turned his attention back to the soup on the stove.

Gil started munching immediately. "You or her?"

"It was me," Chris said. "Just needed some time to sort things out."

"You were together awhile, right?"

"A year."

"Awhile back, your mom told me you were planning a wedding for the spring."

Chris shook his head and smiled. "Mom's not much for secrets, is she?"

"Well, it sure was risky—her letting me know. Why, your secret could've gotten out all over the thriving metropolis of Lewisville. Might've even made the paper!" Gil waited for Chris to chuckle, but the laugh didn't come. "Come on, you two were engaged. It's not like we wouldn't expect a wedding soon."

"It just didn't feel right, Gramps." The soup was beginning to make that wheezing sound before it starts to boil.

"She sure did like you," Gil said.

"Did she tell you that?"

"I saw the way she looked at you last time you were here. It was painted all over her face. That and the way she showed off that ring."

"Did it look like I liked her?"

"Sure did."

"Well, that's because I did. Still do. I guess."

"Listen, Chris. I don't want to pry. But I want you to know you've got an open door to talk to me anytime. About anything."

"I know, Gramps," Chris said.

HE TURNED THE STOVE OFF and moved the pot to the other burner. "When did you know Grandma was right for you?"

"We had a rocky start. About the time I found her, God found me."

"You weren't a Christian yet? I thought all that happened early."

"Not early enough." Gil sighed. "I was nineteen. Your grandmother is the one who converted early. I always did envy those extra years she had with King Jesus."

"How old was she?"

"Maybe seven or eight. She never did have a strong memory of the moment."

"Did that bother her any?"

"Not really. She liked to say, 'You don't have to know the precise moment the sun came up to see it shining.'"

Chris filled up two bowls of soup and took a seat at the table. "Nineteen is kind of late for someone who grew up in church."

"Mom was Methodist. Dad was Baptist. We went to a Presbyterian church off and on for a few years but finally settled in with the Baptists. Life was hard then. Both of them got devout later in life."

"So what made you become a Christian when you were nineteen?"

"Well, I reckon the seeds were planted in my second year of college. Mom and Dad thought I had a future in academics, me being such a reader and all. So I went. I majored in English. Got introduced to good literature—Dickens, Shakespeare, Milton, Chaucer. I felt my mind expanding with each book I read. It was a thrilling time."

The food was sitting on the table, soup steaming. Gil looked it over and then announced to Chris, "I suggest we pray before we eat."

Chris grinned and poked Gil's shoulder. "You've already been munching on the crackers."

"Nothing wrong with that! Best way to express your gratitude to the Lord is to jump right in and start eating."

"You don't say?"

"Of course. Kids don't say thank you before they open presents on Christmas, do they?" Gil laughed. Then he put his hand on top of his grandson's and prayed. "Father, thank You for Your kindness to us today, for bringing us together, for preserving us, for loving us, and for allowing us to enjoy this journey together. Thank You also for this meal. In the name of King Jesus, amen."

When Gil finished, he lifted his head and raised a spoonful of soup to his lips. "A little too hot," he said.

Chris jumped up and went to the freezer, grabbed a couple of ice cubes, and dropped them into the bowls.

Gil noticed Chris was trying to hide a smile. "What's so funny?" he asked.

"Well, Gramps. It's hard for me to picture you as an English major. You know, with your strong southern accent and all."

Gil laughed. And instantly he began speaking with a strong English accent. "When you've got a British accent, people think you're smarter than you are. When you've got a southern accent, people think you're not as smart as you are. But no matter."

Chris's eyes got big. He looked surprised at Gil's voice change.

Gil continued with the fake English accent. "If you're a missionary someplace, you must master the dialect, right? When I came to Lewisville from St. Louis in my twenties, I embraced the accent. It was part of being a good missionary."

Chris shook his head and smiled.

"Are you so surprised?"

"I'd never heard you speak any other way, that's all," Chris said. "I guess I shouldn't be surprised, though. You're a pretty intentional person."

Gil returned to his default southern cadence. "I hope that's a compliment," he said. The ice cube in the soup made a popping sound. Gil stirred it in to help it melt quickly.

"What were you going to do with an English major?"

"I was convinced I'd turn out to be a literary genius. One day people would be analyzing my work, just as I was analyzing the literary greats."

Chris couldn't help but laugh.

"I'm serious," Gil said with a smile. "I wanted immortality. The only way I thought I could attain it was through the written word.

Problem was, I wanted significance, and so I treated people as though they were insignificant. I used people, Chris." At this Gil bowed his head. His voice got soft as he said it again. "I used people."

Gil was remembering a fellow student he befriended in college, thinking he was related to the provost. Once Gil realized he was just an ordinary student with no strings to pull in the upper echelons of academia, he blew him off, even stopped returning his phone calls. He still felt badly about it.

"I loved myself and used people to push myself forward. Had I been a Christian, I would've loved God and used myself to push others forward."

GIL FELT UNCOMFORTABLE at his own confession. This was all in the past. So he decided to get on with the story. "And that's when I met Frances." He pulled one of the framed photos on the tabletop nearer to Chris. It showed him and Frances in their younger years, a formal studio picture.

"She was already a Christian, you said."

"Oh yes. But that didn't matter to me one way or the other at the time. A friend introduced us. She carried herself in a way that said she knew who she was. She didn't have anything to prove to anyone. I liked that."

"When did you start dating Grandma?"

"Well, at first she wasn't interested in going out with me."

"Why not?" Chris was finishing his soup. He pointed to the portrait. "She may have been the beauty in the family, but you weren't too bad yourself."

"The first time I asked her out, she flat turned me down. No hesitation at all. I asked why. So she filled me in. I just wasn't right for her, and we didn't share the same beliefs. That was that."

"Wow."

"I still remember the way she turned me down. She made it clear it was about her, not me, as if I knew the difference."

Chris nodded. "Sometimes I don't know what's worse. Being the one rejected or being the one to reject."

Gil had little doubt he was thinking about Ashley. *Don't pry.*

"Well," Chris said, "I guess I know the end of the story. I wouldn't be here if you and Grandma hadn't figured out a way to make it work."

"I didn't have a clue how to make it work. I thought she was looking for a man to settle down with and take care of her. Someone religious, who'd lead a good moral life. So that was my strategy—get a little religion."

Chris laughed. "It's hard for me to imagine you as 'a little religious.' You've never been 'a little' of anything."

"You're right about that. Being measured and balanced hasn't been my strong point."

"But you've made up for that in passion," Chris said.

"Something like that," Gil said.

"So…the old 'bad guy conversion' trick, huh? You settled down, repented of your wayward ways, and started going to church with Grandma."

"She would've seen through that. I had to convince her I was decent. The real deal. An upstanding Christian gentleman. So I started going to another church—Grace Tabernacle. This was all back in St. Louis. I met with the pastor and told him I wanted to get my act together and start living like a Christian."

"Did he help?"

"Yes and no. He helped me learn some of the basics of Christian living, but he assumed I was already a true believer. He was wrong. So the whole time I was going to that church, it was like trying to stick fruit on the branches of a dead tree. It wasn't organic. There was no life in me."

"I'm guessing Grandma didn't buy your new persona."

"No, she didn't. And I couldn't figure out what it was she wanted. Worst thing about it—she went with Anthony, a guy I knew who was a wolf. A real heel."

Chris's eyes got wide.

Gil continued. "Well, this Anthony fellow got religious all of a sudden—actually, he truly became a Christian—and she gave *him* some thought."

"Did you get mad?"

"No, just frustrated. Here I was, trying to be good enough for Frances. And this clown I used to pal around with gets a chance with her. I thought, 'This isn't fair. I've been acting like a Christian longer than he has, but it's not good enough for her.'"

Chris stacked the bowls and took them to the sink. "You were jealous!"

"I was mad because life wasn't working out like I thought it should." Gil pounded his fist on the table to make the point. "It wasn't because Frances didn't like *me*. I could've lived with that all right. It was that she liked *him*. It didn't make any sense."

"The fact that she would choose another guy over you?"

"No, the fact she would give any attention to a guy who so obviously didn't deserve her. Ironic, isn't it? I didn't get it. This whole business of undeserved favor was the heart of the Christianity I was trying my best to conform to." Gil sighed. "It'd be funny if not for the fact that a lot of people see Christianity the same way."

"What way?"

"That it's just about being and doing good. That it's all about the dos and don'ts."

"You think that's common?" Chris took his place at the table again.

"Almost everyone I've led to Christ—whether they were upstanding, good, moral people or out-and-out scoundrels without a hope in the world—they've all thought, at least at first, that the point of Christianity was 'being good.'"

"That is part of being a Christian, isn't it?"

"Sure. Doctrine of sanctification. God remakes us in the image of Christ. So, yes, we'll grow and become better than we were. But if you think the whole point of Christianity is moral reformation, you'll find out quickly how powerless you are to make that reformation happen."

"So Christianity is about giving up?"

"No, it's about giving *in*," Gil said. "Giving in to God. Handing your heart and life over to Him and casting yourself on His mercy alone."

"And you were trying to become a better person all by yourself—"

"As if I could muster up the power to change. But salvation doesn't come from our willpower. It's God's will and power. Grace comes first."

"So what happened? Did you confront Grandma about how unfair it was?"

"Your grandmother wasn't one you'd want to confront. She'd win. So I just moped around and muttered about it for a couple of weeks. She stopped seeing Anthony, anyway."

"What did you do?"

"I sought him out to see how things had gone. I couldn't confront her, but I could confront him."

"I bet that was a showdown. Did it come to blows?" The look on Chris's face showed he was teasing.

Gil laughed. "The only blow was to my pride. I asked Anthony why things hadn't gone well with Frances. He told me they weren't a fit. Simple as that. Then I asked him why Frances wouldn't go out with me. He told me he didn't know. They never talked about me. That hurt. She wasn't thinking about me nearly as much as I was thinking about her."

"So you didn't learn much from that, huh?"

"Not about Frances, no. But I learned some things about true Christianity."

"From Anthony?"

"Yep. We got to talking about his faith. And I noticed right away how different his view was, compared to mine. I was focused on cleaning myself up and making myself good enough for God, good enough for Frances, good enough for the world. But Anthony didn't talk like that. He kept talking about God being good. About Christ being good enough. About how he wanted to live for God because of what God had done for him. My focus was all on me. His focus was all on God."

Chris nodded his head and stared off toward the window above the sink. Gil wondered what he was thinking.

"It was a couple of months after going to church that I started reading the Bible. Anthony told me to pick a gospel. So I did. The gospel of Mark—it being the shortest, of course. I read it over and over again. I was starting it again one morning, and I got to the place where Jesus was baptized and the Father spoke words over Him, saying, 'Thou art my beloved Son, in whom I am well pleased.' And everything I was hearing in church, from Frances, from Anthony—all of it came together."

"The baptism story?" Chris looked puzzled. "That's an odd part of Scripture for a conversion story."

"The Word's powerful, sharper than a two-edged sword. Even the long lists of names remind you of the faithfulness of God, from generation to generation."

"What about the baptism story got to you?" Chris seemed curious.

"Well, right then I realized all this talk about trusting Jesus and being a true child of God meant that whatever God said about His Son, He could say about me. He loved *me*—Gilbert Walker! Not because I was smart or special or had great talents or gifts. It wasn't because I was living the 'good Christian life' I was trying so hard to get right. He just looked at me and loved me. He delighted in me like a father delighting in his children. It suddenly all made sense."

Gil felt his eyes moistening, but his voice sounded stronger than it had all evening.

"And I saw how deep my sin was. How foolish I was to try and fix myself. How silly my attempts at being a good man looked compared to King Jesus. And then I saw grace. I could look through Jesus's righteousness and hear God say, 'You are My beloved son, Gil. In you I am well pleased.' And here I hadn't even done anything. Hadn't lived right. Hadn't loved right. Hadn't even had the right motive for going to church and reading my Bible. But He loved me anyway. Loved me when I was prideful and self-righteous and using people. Loved me when I was trying my best to earn His approval."

Gil's voice cracked, but he quickly recovered. "And the tears started just rolling down my cheeks. I knelt down by my bed, confessed every sin I could think of, and I just said over and over again, 'Thank You, Jesus. I'm Yours, Jesus. Whatever You want, Jesus.' And in the back of my mind, I heard God's voice clear as day, like an echo in a canyon: 'I delight in you, Gil, just because you're Mine. You belong to Me. I love you as I love My Son.' And right then and there, I knew God accepted me because of Jesus."

Chris took a deep breath and nodded. "Sounds like you got ahold of grace."

"No," Gil said, taking off his glasses and wiping his eyes. "Grace got ahold of me."

The dishes were put up and the kitchen table was clear. Chris said, "It's getting late, Gramps. When do you want to go to bed?"

The question was innocent enough, but it bothered Gil. He wasn't a child who needed to be tucked in.

Before Gil could answer, Chris asked another question. "What's the plan for tomorrow?"

"Plan?" Gil said. Not having a plan was another reminder of his homebound state. "Tomorrow's New Year's Eve. The nurse will be stopping by in the afternoon. That is, if she decides to brave the ice and snow. Other than that, I don't have much of an agenda. It's a shame we can't make it to church."

Chris said, "I'm okay with a quiet day, Gramps. I could use one." Then he walked out of the kitchen and down the hall to the laundry room next to the back door. Gil could hear things clanking around in there.

"What are you looking for?"

Chris's muffled voice barely made it through the wall. "A snow shovel."

"What in the world for?"

The clanking stopped and Chris appeared at the doorway to the kitchen again. "I'm going to shovel the sidewalk tonight so the nurse won't have any trouble tomorrow. Nearly killed myself trying to walk up the drive today. We're lucky your friend Ron didn't slip and fall tonight."

"That's kind of you," Gil said. "But it can wait until morning."

"There's no way I can sleep right now after that long nap. So I might as well get some of my energy out."

Must be wonderful to have energy to spare. "All right, then. We'll shovel the driveway."

"We?" Chris cocked an eyebrow.

"Yes, *we*," Gil said. "As in, you do the shoveling and I'll sit on the porch swing and keep you company. I'm not going to let my house-guest do that kind of work all by himself."

"It can't be more than twenty-five degrees outside. This isn't front-porch weather."

"True. But the porch light went out a couple of weeks ago, and I don't have a spare bulb on hand. The streetlight doesn't reach the sidewalk and driveway. So unless you want to shovel in darkness, I suggest you let me sit on the swing and shine a lantern on you while you're working."

"I can manage in the dark."

"Why manage in the dark when you can thrive in the light?"

FIVE MINUTES LATER, GIL WAS bundled up in a thick black overcoat with gloves, scarf, and hood. Everything except his face was covered. Chris helped him out the door and over to the porch swing. Once Gil's weight landed on the swing, it rocked violently a time or two before Chris steadied it and handed him the big lantern. Gil set it on his lap and pointed it toward the sidewalk and driveway.

Chris got to work shoveling the drive. Within moments, Gil saw him using the shovel as a hammer to chip the ice before pushing it off to the side.

When Chris took a breather, Gil said, "Not easy, is it?"

"Not as easy as snow, that's for sure."

Gil introduced a topic that had been on his mind. "So tell me about this new church you're helping start."

"You know about that?" Chris said.

"Your mother," Gil said. "She said you were talking about being one of the leaders but you were second-guessing yourself."

"Is she using you to pump me for information?" Chris said, only half joking.

Gil thought he'd have a little fun. "Oh, you're on to us now, boy! We mapped out this whole weekend just to get you to spill your guts. You are too quick."

Chris was laughing and breathing hard as he hammered away at the ice. "She's right that I've backed off. I'm not sure I want to commit."

"It sounds like that's common with you."

Chris stopped shoveling for a moment and looked away. "You, uh, you make it sound as though it's bad to be sure of something before committing," he said.

"I never said that's a bad thing. It's just that she said you're looking into a master's in religious studies."

"So?"

"So it seems a little strange to me that you just finished college but want to take some more classes about religion, while at the same time you're backing away from church."

Chris was grunting as he chipped at the ice.

Gil worried he may have overstepped. "Am I wrong to be a little puzzled?"

Chris stopped chipping the ice and leaned on the shovel. "That's a fair question, I guess."

"Last time you were here, you didn't say anything about your study plans."

"Well, I was just starting to think about it. Besides, we were a little busy with the funeral, Gramps," Chris said. "Didn't seem like the best time to update you on my educational pursuits."

Gil wasn't sure, but the way Chris said "educational pursuits" sounded sarcastic. It wasn't normally the way Chris talked. Gil felt he'd hit a nerve.

"Okay, okay. I've just never heard you talk about being in ministry."

"Who said I wanted to be in ministry?"

"Well, I just assumed that's why you'd do religious studies. A professor, then? A missionary?"

"Not sure what I'll end up as," Chris said. "Probably a professor." He spent a few minutes chipping at the ice before pushing back his hood. He was cold and sweaty at the same time. "You don't happen to have a pickax, do you? It'd be a lot easier than trying to break up this ice with a snow shovel."

"There's one in the barn around back," Gil said. "Here, take the light."

Once Chris had trudged off to the back of the house with the lantern, Gil looked from under the porch's eaves at the night sky. The clouds that had been present all day had vanished. In the absence of a moon, the stars stood out in a bright glitter.

Gil then noticed just how cold it was. He breathed in a lungful of chilled air, then exhaled slowly, watching the fog of his breath in front of him. For the first time, Gil felt worried about his grandson—and not just about his love life.

CHRIS SHONE THE LANTERN LIGHT inside the old barn as he sorted through some of Gil's old tools. As he did so, he thought about the direction this conversation was going. At first, he had been happy to talk about his plan to take some religion classes. He thought this would satisfy Gil and perhaps keep them from delving into the bigger issues surrounding Chris's faith. But now Gil was probing into his motivations, and Chris wasn't sure he liked it.

Once Chris spotted the pickax, he grabbed it and stepped back outside. He took a minute to look up and notice the soundless twinkling of the stars all over the sky. Instead of looking beautiful to him, the night sky seemed immense and cold. It made him feel small.

Chris trudged back toward the driveway, the snow and ice crunching beneath his shoes. He handed the lantern back to Gil and held up the pickax. "This will be so much easier!" He pulled his hood back over his head.

Gil resumed their conversation immediately. "I didn't mean to pry earlier. But I was a little surprised when your mother told me about your plans."

"Well, Gramps, I'm curious. You know how much I like discussing theology with you. Studying it is a hobby. And I love to debate." Back in safe territory now.

Chris returned to the driveway and put the pickax to good use. The ice was breaking up much more easily now. He was halfway finished with the driveway in just a few minutes. Looking over his work, he stopped to catch his breath.

"What is it about studying theology that appeals to you?" Gil said.

Chris had a stock answer for that one. "Society is full of people with competing ideas. Big questions about God, the world, evil, forgiveness—all of these are theological questions. And then there's the history of theology and the problems the church has caused through the years. Theology matters."

"Oh, it does, it does." Gil was rocking slightly on the swing, but not so much that the lantern didn't stay focused on Chris's work. "But what's your ultimate goal? Why do you want to do it?"

Chris hammered away at the ice for a couple more minutes as he mulled over Gil's question. *Why? Why does it matter why?* Finally he stopped and gave an answer. "I guess... Well, I want to know why people do the things they do. Why churches take the positions they do. Why wars are fought over God and religion. Why so many people claim to believe something but don't live it out. I want to wrestle with the big questions of life."

"All well and good," said Gil. "But where do you want to end up?"

"Where do I want to live?"

"No," Gil said. "I mean, where do you want all that wrestling to get you?"

Gil was asking the same question over and over again. Chris was afraid he was being caught in an inconsistency. Here he was, fresh out of college, almost ready to walk away from the faith at the same time he was thinking about getting a religious education.

Chris tried to dodge the question. "I don't need to get anywhere. If I finish these classes with a little more understanding of myself and this world, then it'll be worth it, right? The joy is in the journey, not the destination."

Gil was quiet for a few moments. Chris kept working. After a couple of minutes, he decided to turn the tables. "Why did *you* go to seminary?" He stopped chipping the ice so he could hear Gil's response.

"Well, for some of the same reasons. I'm a little curious too. You probably get that from me. And I wanted to learn more about why I' believe what I believe, and why it matters. I'm a lifelong learner, and yes, there's joy in the journey..." he said, his voice trailing off.

"But?"

"I don't think it's enough to do theology just to wrestle with life's big questions," Gil said.

"Why not?"

"Because theology is personal. We're not talking about some abstract thought. Of course, you learn a lot about the world and about yourself when you study theology. But the goal is to know more about God so that you come to know Him better."

I should have known he would go there, Chris thought. "So that's why you went to seminary? To know God? Isn't that what church is for?" Chris asked. "You don't have to get a degree to know God. Even you've said that before."

"Oh, I know," Gil said. "I just think that, for the Christian, anytime we take up theology, it ought to be rooted in love for God. And that's what'll help us better serve the church. I'd say the same thing to any thinking Christian who's wrestling with the truth about God, not just to a religion student."

Though Chris shared Gil's interest in theology, he realized they were coming from two different worlds. Chris thought back to his classes with Dr. Coleman and the conversations they'd had about the weaknesses of traditional Christianity and how many convictional

Christians were just hypocrites whose anti-intellectualism impeded progress in the world.

"That kind of education is focused on boundaries. It suppresses innovation. It stops progress. We need academic freedom and experimentation. A fresh view of things! If I went to seminary for the same reasons you did when you were my age, I'd wind up with all my initial beliefs confirmed rather than challenged. I want to be open-minded."

"As long as you realize the point of having an open mind."

"What do you mean by that?"

"An open mind is like an open mouth. It's meant to close on something. We ought to make sure it's on something good."

"I don't think it's ever good to have a closed mind." Chris was done chipping ice. He threw down the pickax and picked up the snow shovel. "A closed mind stunts intellectual growth."

"Oh, really?" Gil said. He chuckled. "You just think about that for a minute."

Chris couldn't tell if he was hot because of his work or because he didn't like the way the conversation was going. Maybe both. But he wasn't about to let his granddad get away with such a silly statement. "I don't have to think about it, Gramps. Closed-mindedness is the root of religious conflict. Closed-mindedness causes all sorts of problems in the world. It's because people stopped thinking and started following blindly that the world has gotten into the shape it's in."

"Is that so?" Gil said.

"Of course. People are so stubborn, especially from our church background. They think they know everything. And then they're hypocritical because they don't live up to the standards they set for themselves." Chris was thinking about his dad, but he didn't say so. "Our biggest weakness is that people are closed-minded."

Gil grunted his disapproval. "You say a closed mind stunts intellectual growth. I say that a closed mind is the only thing that enables intellectual growth."

Chris cocked an eyebrow to put his skepticism on full display.

Gil went on. "In fact, I'd go even further than that. Your intellectual growth depends on becoming *more* closed-minded, just as long as your mind is closing in on the truth."

Chris leaned against the shovel and pulled down his hood again, as if to physically express his disbelief. "Did I hear you right? Are you saying I should be closed-minded?"

Gil was obviously unfazed. "Think back to kindergarten. Your teacher goes over numbers with you. Until you agree to the basics, like two plus two equals four, you never move on to the multiplication tables. And if you stay endlessly open-minded and never accept the truth that five times five equals twenty-five, then you'll never be able to do an advanced math problem. Not to mention calculus!" Gil stifled a chuckle and muttered under his breath, "Only God knows how I ever passed that class." Then he finished. "You've got to accept basic truths before you can grow into deeper and richer truths."

"That works fine if you're talking about facts and math and science and stuff. But we're talking about religion, Gramps. Religion. Theology. World-view stuff. Religion has to do with values and ideas and opinions. It's not the same thing as adding and subtracting."

Gil tapped his fingers on the lantern, apparently waiting for Chris to finish.

"Too many Christians think about truth the way you do—that it's just a bunch of facts that can be proved or disproved. But a lot of people think the Bible may be pointing us to a richer and deeper idea of truth, one that moves beyond facts. Truth based on someone's place and situation. It's a more complex understanding of truth." Chris knew he sounded condescending, but he figured Gil wouldn't mind. That was par for the course when discussing issues of great importance.

"Your view of truth and Christianity makes good sense in society today."

"Thank you," Chris said. He shoveled the last of the snow down the walk and then turned back to his grandfather, as if he'd won the argument.

"I didn't mean it as a compliment," Gil said. "I didn't mean it as an insult either, just a statement of fact. Unless you don't believe in that kind of fact."

Chris pointed his finger at his granddad and grinned.

"What I mean to say is that your view of Christianity fits fine with how people today think of truth, values, facts, and religion. But it doesn't fit well at all with the way the New Testament talks about these things."

"Why do you say that?" Chris asked.

"For one, you're not taking into account the history at the center of the faith. The gospel is about certain events. Now, either those events happened or they didn't. So I agree with you. Truth can't be reduced to facts, like one plus one equals two. But you can't reduce truth to values and opinions either. As if theology is just about preference, like choosing one flavor of ice cream over another."

"But people disagree on the facts," Chris said. "Some people say these events happened. Other people say they were made up and spread by early Christians. Who is to say who is right and wrong?"

"That is the question, isn't it?"

"Actually, I don't know that it matters all that much. If you happen to believe something is true that didn't happen, and it makes you a better person, then there's no real harm done. What matters is how we live," Chris said, leaning over on the shovel.

That lean turned out to be a mistake. His back foot happened to be resting on a piece of stray ice, and the weight shift turned it into a cartoonish, banana-peel moment where both legs flailed in the air before he landed hard on his backside. He let out an *"Oof!"*

Gil burst into a raspy old-man laugh. Chris quickly stood up, red faced and sweaty, then picked his pride off the ground and eventually joined in the laughing.

"I'm thinking of all kinds of jokes right now, but I'll spare you," Gil said, patting his knees to warm his legs.

"Thanks, Gramps. I appreciate that. Where were we?"

"I was just about to tell you why you are wrong to say it doesn't matter if what we believe didn't happen."

"Of course, go on," Chris said, his words dripping with sarcasm.

"The apostle Paul would disagree with you. First Corinthians 15. If King Jesus has not been raised from the dead, we'd be better off living like everyone else. The whole of Christianity is senseless and pointless." Gil sighed. "And we of all people are the most to be pitied."

"Well," Chris said, still trying to shake the memory of his fall, "even if Paul says the Resurrection is important, I don't see why that means Christians should go around thinking we are the only ones who have the truth. Surely other religions have truth as well," Chris said.

"Certainly," Gil said. "By the grace of God, there is truth to be found everywhere."

"Right. So who is to say that we can find truth in Christianity but not in other religions?" Chris asked.

"Ah, now *you* are the one speaking of truth as if it were just some code of morality that all religions could agree on. And *I* am the one pointing you to a deeper vision of truth, one that is immensely personal."

Chris was frustrated that Gil had turned the tables on him again.

"Truth is not a formula," Gil said, "a moral code that can be discovered in the religions of the world. Truth is a Person. And knowing the truth means knowing God, which brings us back to the point of theology, anyway."

"All I'm saying is maybe other religions help us know different aspects of who God is."

"That makes sense," said Gil, to Chris's surprise, but then he continued, "until you actually study the other religions. Then you find out just how different they are."

"I've been studying other religions, Gramps. Had a class in college on world religions this last semester. And the professor proved there is a moral code common to all of them. That's why even our celebrations are similar."

"Give me an example," Gil said.

Chris racked his brain, trying to remember the notes he took from Dr. Coleman's lectures on moral behavior in the world religions. He remembered enough of the main themes to get his point across. "Take the spring celebrations. Passover comes during springtime. The Jews celebrate their freedom from slavery. It's a celebration of humans breaking the chains of bondage. Inspiring, really. A demonstration of the unbreakable nature of the human spirit and the longing for freedom we all share."

"Go on," said Gil.

"Easter's the same thing. The triumph of the human spirit. Just think—here is Jesus standing up against the oppression of the Roman Empire, and after His death, His movement is carried on by His disciples until it outlasts even Caesar's reign."

Gil cocked an eyebrow and then interrupted. "And I suppose you're going to talk about how Islam celebrates the binding of Isaac, and how submission is the path to human greatness, right?"

Chris didn't respond, but he was thinking to himself, *How did he know?*

Gil chuckled. "Pious poppycock," he said quietly.

"How's that?"

"Pious poppycock," Gil said again, louder. Seeing that Chris had finished shoveling the walk, Gil scooted over on the porch swing to make room for him.

Chris made no move.

"No, come here," insisted Gil.

Chris unwrapped his scarf and took a seat next to his grandfather.

Gil put his arm around him. "Do you think any practicing Jew, Christian, or Muslim would be okay with how you just described those events? What you've just done, my boy, is given me three holy days with a twenty-first-century multifaith spin. In the process, you've failed to be true to any one of them. Any self-respecting Jew, Christian, or Muslim should protest you for patronizing them that way."

"I'm not patronizing," Chris said. "I'm showing they all celebrate the same thing."

"Well, they don't," Gil said matter-of-factly. "What Christian thinks that Easter is just the commemoration of a man who stood against the empire? Nonsense! Easter is about the vindication of the Son of God. He took our sins upon Himself when He died upon the cross. It's about the beginning of God's new creation. Jesus Christ being exalted as the risen King and Lord of the world."

"But I didn't say—"

"And faithful Jews don't see Passover as the triumph of the human spirit. For pity's sake. It's the mighty hand of God rescuing His people and enacting justice. It's God who acts in the Exodus. It's God who smites the mighty Pharaoh. It's God who drowns the Egyptian army. The children of Israel are cowering and afraid. Even Moses is afraid to stutter before Pharaoh! But God calls out His people. He delivers them and displays His glory so that everyone would know He is the *one true* God." Gil slowed down and emphasized the "one true" part.

Chris realized his granddad had slipped into preaching mode, but he knew there was no use fighting it. Once a preacher, always a preacher.

"I never said they were all the same." Chris was backtracking now. "I just said there was a common morality behind the religions. You can find people with different religious beliefs working in orphanages and helping the poor. And I say that as long as the end result is the same—people loving their neighbors—then I'm not sure if what anybody believes matters all that much."

Gil took a deep breath and patted Chris on the shoulder. "Well, Chris, if religion is all about making the world a better place and treating people nicely, then I suppose you're right. Distinctive religious beliefs don't matter too much."

He turned away from Chris and fiddled with the lantern buttons until the light went out.

WITH THE LIGHT EXTINGUISHED, it suddenly felt colder. Chris was stunned by how the conversation had ended. Neither one of them had ever given up an argument before, yet it seemed that's what his grandfather had just done.

"Well, I'm glad we agree on something," Chris said softly. He stood up from the porch swing, took the lantern to the front door, and bent down to untie his shoes. A few moments later, he opened the front door and turned to Gil. "I find it hard to believe you have nothing more to say, Gramps."

Gil, still seated in the porch swing, looked up at him and smiled. "What? You're surprised I agreed with you?"

"Well...yes, as a matter of fact."

Gil steadied himself on the porch swing and started to stand up. Chris rushed over to help him. The light from the living room spilled out of the windows and made the wooden planks of the porch glow. Gil then made his way toward the door, moving stiffly. "You said if religion is all about people being nice, then distinctive beliefs don't matter."

"Right," Chris said, "and you agreed."

"Of course," said Gil. "*If* that's what religion is all about—ethics. But that's a pretty big 'if,' I think. My friend Tim, who doesn't believe in God, would be offended."

"You have a friend who is an atheist?" Chris was surprised.

"Several, actually," Gil replied. "Although I'm not sure they'd all say they're atheists. Some would rather say they're agnostic about the existence of God. Truth be told, the only thing my atheist friends are sure about is that they don't like the God they don't believe in."

"But why would they be offended at what I said? That religion is about ethics?" Chris was genuinely curious.

"Because they have no religion. But they still believe in ethics. You see, when you reduce religion to ethics, you insult the nonreligious, ethical people in the world," Gil said. "People like Tim."

"I don't mean to insult anyone, Gramps."

"But that's what happens when you shrink Christianity down to mere religion. And then you shrink religion down to a system of morals. Are you sure that your 'if' doesn't require a larger leap of faith than mine?"

Chris opened the door to let them both in.

"All right, then. What is your 'if'?" Chris asked. He sent the deadbolt home. Then he and his grandfather began removing their outer layers of clothing.

"What if Christianity is bigger than ethics?" Gil asked. "What if it's not about good people getting better but about dead people coming to life? What if it's not about man seeking God but God seeking man? What if it's not about how people view God but how God views us? What if Christianity isn't about you and me and everyone else in the first place? Those are the questions I hope you ask. They're worth wrestling with."

Chris was about to say something, but before he could put his thoughts together, his grandfather put his hand on his shoulder from behind. "Chris, make sure you don't use scholarship as a way of masking your doubts, of defending yourself against the Bible, of distancing yourself from God's claim on your life."

Once that message was delivered, Chris felt totally exposed, as if Gil had seen through all his religious activity to the deadness of his heart.

For a moment or two, Chris wondered how he should respond. He turned back toward his grandfather and saw him smile gently. This conversation was over. "What time do you go to bed, Gramps?"

"Oh, about eight thirty or so. Except when I get a little wild and stay up until nine."

Chris laughed. "Well, then we're past your bedtime. I'm going to take a quick shower. I feel gross from being in the car so much today."

"Not to mention rolling all over the ground out there tonight," Gil said with a wink.

Chris didn't take long in the shower. The upstairs bathroom was a converted storage space with a sloping ceiling he frequently bumped his head on. The tiles were cold, sending chills up his legs, and the water pressure was pitiful.

While trying to stay under the trickling stream of warm water, he thought about his granddad. The two of them didn't always see eye to eye, but Chris was sure of one thing—Gil's affection for him. His grandfather reassured Chris of his love consistently, as if to make sure he would never forget. Or as if to try to make up for his father's absence.

Deep down, Chris was both attracted to and repelled by Gil's firm convictions. The two of them were like a couple of magnets, drawn together or pushed apart as the alignment of their charges shifted.

Once he finished his shower, Chris dried off and threw on a clean pair of sweatpants and a T-shirt.

To make sure Gil was okay, Chris tiptoed down the stairs, trying to keep the planks from creaking under him. But when he saw light coming from underneath the door to Gil's bedroom, he knocked. Gil was sitting up in his bed with the lamp on, reading his Bible.

"You okay, Gramps?"

Chris saw moisture in his eyes. Gil offered a sad smile. "Yes, fine…fine," Gil said.

Chris noticed that Gil had laid pillows down the length of the opposite side of the bed. A heartbreaking place keeper.

"I'm sorry," Chris said awkwardly.

Gil smiled at him again and wiped his left eye.

"This is the hardest part," Gil said. "Even still. I can't seem to sleep well without something against my back."

"I can't imagine," Chris said, putting his hands in his pockets and rocking back.

"Fifty-six years. Fifty-six wonderful years my angel slept right beside me."

"I know," Chris said, nodding his head in agreement.

"Yes," Gil said. "It helps to read my Bible until I fall asleep. 'Thy word is a lamp unto my feet.' I've never felt the truth of that more than now."

"You were a great husband," Chris said. "I'm proud of you. Never seen another man love a woman quite like that."

"Oh, I was a rotten husband a lot of the time, but I did love her. That much is for sure." He began nodding and looking off in the distance.

Chris walked over and hugged him. He whispered, "I miss her too."

"I'm about to turn off my light and look out the window at starlight on the snow. That's a beautiful sight, and it's not every day we get to see it."

"Get some rest," Chris said.

BACK UPSTAIRS IN HIS BEDROOM, Chris went over to the window seat and opened the shades, looking out over the hill and the stately oak trees sagging under the weight of the ice. A couple of branches had already snapped and were lying on the ground. He thought of his granddad one floor below, looking out his own window and finding beauty. *Must be in the eye of the beholder,* he thought. Everything looked dark and empty to Chris. He pulled the shades and clambered into bed.

His door was still open, and the light from the night-light in the hall palely illuminated his room. He stared at the ceiling, counting the cracks that ran through the paneling, places where the house had settled over the years. He turned to one side and examined the wallpaper, a mixture of flowers and musical notes. *Reminds me of Grandma,* he thought. *Flowers and music. Beauty and joy.*

After his long nap in the afternoon, and his stimulating discussion with his granddad, going to sleep that night proved to be a struggle. He tried to turn his mind off but couldn't.

What if Gramps is right and Dr. Coleman is wrong? What if having an open mind is a mistake if it means we're failing to close our minds around something that is true? But then if Christianity is true, why does it produce so much bigotry, so much hatred even?

He thought about Luke and Cami, Ashley, his mom. *They've got it all together. They know what they believe, and they think it will change the world. I want to believe again. I want to be like them. But I don't want blind belief. And I don't want a faith that is us-against-them. I don't want to be a hypocrite like Dad. Better to let down Mom or Grandpa by telling the truth than by faking my faith.*

Chris lifted his head and then a moment later slammed it back down into his pillow. His insides ached, partly from exhaustion after all the shoveling, partly from the weariness in his soul.

Oh, God, he sighed. He wasn't swearing. Nor was he praying. It was something in between. Never before had God seemed so distant.

This made him remember a time that had been so different.

It was in this very house almost a decade earlier, when Chris was thirteen, that he felt God's presence in a unique and powerful way.

He spent a week with his grandparents that summer. One day, all day long, he helped Gil out in the barn. They cut the grass and put mulch in the flower bed that surrounded the front porch. Chris must have rolled down the hill a dozen times. Grandma Frances made a big supper for them, meat and potatoes, after a long day of work that seemed more like fun.

Chris's grandparents used to like having friends and neighbors over for an informal jam session. Musicians and singers, and those who couldn't sing but thought they could, filled up the front porch, front room, and dining room for a rowdy night of song and dance. Country-and-western, bluegrass, "old-timey music," hymns, gospel. They did it all. Not all the songs were spiritual songs, but all the people were spiritual people, and Chris recalled how he experienced the presence of God that night they all sang.

Chris recalled, too, how the concert seemed to go on after he went to bed. With the windows open, he could hear all the sounds of the summer night harmonizing in a glorious symphony of praise. The crickets provided a steady tone in the background, with the frogs a half mile down at the river croaking out a steady rhythm. As the night breeze would sweep through the yard, the stately oaks on one side of the hill would start to ruffle their leaves, and slowly but surely the ruffling would spread to all the other trees, as if they had conferred together and decided to applaud Jesus. Nature seemed electrified in how it sparked Chris's sense of wonder.

That night he sensed the heavenly sweetness of Christ's love. God had never seemed closer. It was as if a glow of divine love had come from Jesus Himself, into his heart, like a stream of sweet light. On that night he began to get chill bumps all over his body. They started at the top of his head and moved all the way down to the tips of his toes. *God loves me. God loves me. He really loves me.* Wave after wave of God's love seemed to wash over him. The kindness of God was so palpable, so present, the sense that God was *for* him so real that all Chris could do was smile, close his eyes, and rest in the beauty of grace.

But that was a long time ago. It was winter now. There were no sounds of life outside. And Chris couldn't detect any signs of life in his own heart. The world seemed dead to him and he to the world. He lay on the bed, staring at the ceiling, the cracks staring back at him, mirroring the foundations of his faith. For some reason, the reminder of the joy he had known as a boy made him weary. Whatever wonder he had experienced in that house a decade earlier was now buried beneath winter's fury. He felt a deep sense of loss, quieter than words, drier than tears.

Chris was drifting in and out of memories now until his feeling of loss reminded him of another day. An unassuming day. One that turned out to forever draw a line between "before" and "after."

It was the fall of the same year he had felt God's presence so strongly. He was in his childhood home in nearby Crossville, watching out the window as his father packed the last of his things in the trunk of the car. His mother appeared behind him and placed her hand on his shoulder. He pulled away and left the room. It was her fault! She was the one doing this to Dad, doing this to them both!

His anger melted into tears, and Chris dashed out the front door in his bare feet. Before his dad could react, Chris jumped in the backseat and put on a seat belt.

"No, son," his father said, shaking his head.

"I'm going with you," Chris said adamantly, as if by sheer will-power he could change his future.

"No, you're not." Dad reached in and started fiddling with the seat-belt strap.

Chris resisted, pushed his dad away, and held tight to the belt, using his shoulder to keep himself lodged in the seat. Only a few seconds later, he let go of the belt and was holding tight to his dad as he pulled him out of the car. He wept into his father's scratchy wool sweater, heaving with great sobs and saying over and over again, "I need you. Don't leave me."

Back in the present, Chris sat up in bed, bleary-eyed from fresh tears. *Mom was the one I should have been hugging,* he thought. The revelations of his father's multiple affairs, which he had learned about years later, had turned his world upside down. He'd been lied to, straight in the face, by his saint of a father. He'd always assumed his father was being forced out of the house, when in reality, his mother was being abandoned for one of his dad's many on-the-side women. The horror of the situation was still fresh—not only his father's betrayal and hypocrisy but also the fact that Chris had spent so many years in the dark.

CHRIS GLANCED AT THE CLOCK. 1:15. He had to do something to get his mind out of that never-ending pit, and he knew that continuing to lie in bed was not it. He thought about going downstairs and browsing through Gil's old books to find something to read. *I might wake him up if I go downstairs,* he thought, remembering how loudly the stairs had squeaked.

Chris was pretty sure he could find an old novel in his father's room, which had been left largely unchanged since his father had gone off to college. He sometimes liked reading boys' adventure books even though he was too old for them now. But nothing would induce him to go into his father's room.

What about Aunt Ruth's room? There might be something to read in there.

Chris got out of bed and flipped on the light. He walked across the hall, taking care not to make the old wood floors creak any more than he had to.

He turned on the light in his aunt's room. This room, too, had changed little over the years. There were no books on the room's single shelf, only mementos of a girlhood long gone. But then Chris noticed a small chest, not three feet high, blocking a closet door. *That's funny. As if it's put there to keep you out.* He was too curious not to look. As quietly as he could, he pushed the chest out of the way. He grimaced as the door started to open with a creaking sound. *That's why the chest was there, to hold the door shut.*

He fumbled around for a light switch, then looked into the large closet with its sloping roof. From the rod hung several empty hangers and some old clothes. An exercise bike was stored to one side, next to some boxes of shoes and a peculiar-looking basket of mementos.

Chris pulled out the basket and noticed a three-by-five-inch card taped to the side with his grandmother's handwriting: "Third." Interesting.

He took the basket into the bedroom where the light was better, set it down on the bed, and started looking through its contents. There were lots of photos. People playing guitars and fiddles and harmonicas. Potluck dinners with rotund, pink-cheeked women in their Sunday best, standing behind tables dishing out their specialties. Kids trying to avoid being photographed, hiding behind their parents' legs. Along with the pictures were a couple of plaques of appreciation as well as some old church directories.

Chris realized what "Third" stood for. Third Baptist—the church his granddad had been pastor of for forty years. Gil once told him the history of this small church with a name so ordinary.

"It's not to be confused with the historic First Baptist downtown," he'd said.

"Where is Second Baptist?" Chris had asked.

"No Second Baptist in Lewisville, at least by that name. The official Second Baptist church is Mount Zion." Gil was referring to a well-known African American congregation. "You see, the good folks that planted Third Baptist on the west side of town didn't want to name theirs Second and somehow slight their black brothers and sisters."

"So that's why!"

"Naming it Third also made it less likely there would be another," Gil had said. It made sense. Three Baptist churches provided plenty of choices for a town that barely numbered 1,000 residents and only 250 Baptists. A fourth Baptist church in a town as small as Lewisville was unthinkable.

Gil never boasted of numbers, or anything else for that matter, but Chris's mother had told him that, while he was pastor, Third Baptist had twice as many members as First. They weren't big numbers compared to a city church—only 125 or so. But Gil's leadership of a church that size in a town as small as Lewisville, not to mention his lengthy tenure as pastor, had solidified his reputation in town as a sort of sage. The whole county esteemed him. At one point, Chris found out, he was urged to run for mayor, but he declined, saying his business was with God's people.

Chris didn't remember much about Third Baptist as a kid. But in hearing his mom and grandparents reminisce and tell stories, he was impressed by how well the people knew one another. Really knew one another. Struggles were out in the open. Sin was dealt with privately and publicly. These people loved one another, and their love was tough. There were grudges and catfights and all the kinds of things you expect wherever people live. But through all the stories, Chris could sense the genuine love these people had for one another.

It was a stark contrast with Chris's church experience in the city. In the churches Chris had belonged to, "Love one another" meant "Stay on the surface." Avoid conflict at all cost. So church was full of nice-looking people who smiled at one another, suppressed their disagreements, and for the sake of "unity" made sure that every possible conflict was squashed before it could lead to a difficult situation.

Chris put the church directories back in the basket, arranged the pictures the way he had found them, and then put everything back in the closet. He glanced at the clock again. 2:07. *I ought to get back in bed.*

JUST THEN HIS EYES FELL on another box, peeking out from beneath some old pillowcases. There was another three-by-five-inch card, this one stapled to the side, with one word on it: "Sermons."

Chris tugged at the box, surprised at how much heavier it was compared to the basket of church mementos. Once he dragged it into the bedroom and heaved it up onto the bed, he saw that the box was filled with reams of paper. Notebook paper, yellowed and worn, with faded handwriting on each page. The papers were clipped together in bundles, a card with a year written on each one.

Chris picked up one of the bundles. "1978." As he flipped through the papers, probably 150 or so in the bundle, he realized these were all the sermons Gil had preached at Third that year.

Chris selected a sermon at random. It was dated April 19, 1978. In the right-hand corner was the date, and underneath was Gil's handwriting: "Wed night." The sermon title was "Jesus Versus Popularity." The text was John 6.

Reading through the sermon notes, Chris realized this was a message for the teenagers at Third Baptist. All the illustrations involved situations at high school. Chris read through the one-page sermon outline, filled from top to bottom with text (as if Gil were short on paper at the time). He was impressed by the way his granddad weaved together a message of self-worth ("Who you are in Christ matters more than what people think of you") and self-denial ("Who you are in Christ means people may think badly of you"). The thoughts and phrases scrawled on these papers were rich.

In this particular sermon outline, one name came up three times: Katy. Chris flipped through several other sermons and didn't find any references to names. Apparently something in the youth group must have happened involving a girl named Katy. At the bottom of the page, under her name, was this line: "Don't trust in your strength, because there is such a thing as pride. Don't despair in your weakness, because there is such a thing as forgiveness."

On parts of the page, it was difficult for Chris to make out the handwriting, but there were a couple of quotes that stood out. One read, "You may think you are rebelling by going against your parents. Not so. The true rebellion is in the heart of the Christian who follows King Jesus by swimming upstream against the current of the world." Another quote was written in a different color of ink, sideways on the margin, as if Gil had thought of it later but wanted to include it in his notes: "You may feel alive when you go with the flow, but any old dead thing can float downstream."

He also saw 2 Corinthians 4:6 referenced in parentheses and then this: "The world says, 'Be true to yourself.' King Jesus says, 'Be true to your future self.' "

Chris didn't want to mess with the sermons or get them out of order, but the outline for the youth service with this mysterious Katy intrigued him. So he pulled it out of the binder, taking care not to tear the top of the page. He put it on the nightstand.

Maybe there were other clues. Chris rustled through the basket of mementos again and picked out a couple of church directories from the late 1970s. He flipped through the names and faces, looking for a Katy somewhere.

He found her. In 1975. "Katy Baisley." There she was, a girl with short brown hair and a face filled with freckles. She had on a bright red dress with white polka dots and frilly white lace around her neck. She couldn't have been older than twelve. She was in the picture with her mom and dad and sister, Sarah.

He dug around for another church directory and found one from 1978. The Baisleys were there again, all four of them. Katy had developed into a stunningly beautiful teenage girl.

There wasn't a directory from 1979, but there was one from 1980. He looked up the Baisleys. There they were. But Katy was missing. It was just her parents and Sarah. *Interesting. There's got to be a story there somewhere.* He didn't find another directory until 1985, and there were no Baisleys at all in that one.

He yawned suddenly. The clock said 3:15 now. He was finally getting sleepy.

Chris stowed the box back in the closet, underneath the pillowcases where he had found it. He decided to leave the closet door open, to avoid making any extra noise. He tiptoed across the hall to his own room, turned out the light, and climbed into bed. Enough adventure for one night.

Sunday, December 31

The sun woke up Chris. It was coming into the window at just the right angle to warm his face.

The smell of coffee told Chris that his granddad was up already. *He's probably making breakfast,* he thought, feeling guilty. *Here I am supposed to be helping him this weekend, and he's the one waiting on me!* He pulled back the covers, got up, and stumbled toward the bathroom.

A few minutes later he was dressed for the day. He went downstairs and crossed the hall into the kitchen. There he spotted Gil sitting at the table, an e-reader in hand. The sight caused Chris to do a double take. *Grandpa has a tablet?* Then again, why should he be surprised? No matter how old or feeble Gil was, he seemed determined to not let the world pass him by. Even though the house seemed ancient, Gil had a way of transcending time.

"Morning, Gramps," Chris said.

Gil looked up from the tablet and welcomed Chris to the table. "Morning! Have a seat." He put the e-reader down. "Did you sleep well?"

"Not really," Chris said. "You?"

"Oh, all right, I guess. I like winter nights. When it's cold outside, it makes you appreciate a warm bed. I was secretly hoping an overnight thaw would make the roads and sidewalks safe enough for us to go to church. But that didn't happen."

Chris couldn't keep his eyes off the tablet device. "You've got to tell me the story behind that."

"What story?" asked Gil. Chris could tell he was feigning surprise but knew full well what he was referring to.

"Come on. Don't give me that. You have an e-reader?"

"You think there must be a story. Why? Because I'm old? Out of touch?" Gil said.

"I don't know what you heard, but I didn't say that." Chris laughed.

"I know you didn't. But that's what you were thinking." Gil took off his glasses and picked up the tablet. "It was the only way your mom could convince me to give up the car."

"The car for a tablet?" Chris said. "Bad trade."

"You're telling me!" Gil said, grinning. "No, seriously, when your mom and your aunt Ruth started talking to me about giving up the car, I knew I wouldn't be able to drive into town to visit the library. You know I used to go down there at least once a week. They have a great library loan system going."

He sipped some coffee, and his lips contorted in a way that told Chris he needed more sugar.

"Here you go," Chris said. He grabbed a handful of sugar packets from the counter for Gil.

"Thank you much," Gil said. After a bit of stirring, he continued. "So, when they talked about taking away the car, I asked for a reading device. Something—anything—that could keep me up to date on things. I wanted the ability to get new books without leaving my easy chair."

Chris smiled. A pang in his stomach reminded him about breakfast. "So, what are we having this morning?"

"I don't know. Aren't you the chef?"

"How about scrambled eggs and sausage?"

"That will work."

Gil went back to reading his tablet while Chris whipped up some eggs in one skillet and grilled some sausage in another. It only took a few minutes before the food was ready. There were some oranges in the refrigerator. He sliced a couple of them and put them on a plate.

"What are you reading?"

"I've been working through Augustine's *Confessions* the last few days. I found it for free online. I remember now why I loved it so much."

"A classic, for sure," Chris said. "Isn't it the first autobiography in the modern sense?"

"It's composed as a prayer. But it's an autobiography in a way." Gil picked the tablet back up and began pushing buttons here and there. "So much truth here. Do you want to hear some of my favorite parts?"

"I guess," Chris said. He was dishing out the eggs and sausage onto two plates.

"Augustine was awed by the truth that God reveals Himself to us. Listen here: 'And, when You are poured out on us, You are not thereby brought down; rather, we are uplifted.'"

"Huh," Chris murmured, trying to sound uninterested.

"Listen to this. About his sinful past. 'You were always by me, mercifully angry and flavoring all my unlawful pleasures with bitter discontent, in order that I might seek pleasures free from discontent. But where could I find such pleasure except in You, O Lord—except in You, who teaches us by sorrow, who wounds us to heal us, and kills us, that we might not die apart from You.'"

"Kills us?" Chris was surprised at the rawness of the language, particularly from a book almost seventeen hundred years old.

"Of course," Gil said. "We die with Christ and are raised to new life."

Gil was pushing and swiping on the e-reader, apparently looking for something. "Oh yes, I highlighted this," he said. "When he gets close to his conversion, the struggle gets stronger. He talks about having two wills struggling inside him—one will drawing him to God's love that 'satisfied and vanquished' him and one will pulling him to his own lust that 'pleased and fettered' him. And that struggle brought him face to face with his own sin." Gil began reading out loud again: "'And now You set me face to face with myself, that I might see how ugly I was, and how crooked and sordid, bespotted and ulcerous. And I looked and I loathed myself.'"

"Kind of a downer, huh?" Chris said. He was only half joking.

"I doubt it would be a self-help bestseller today," Gil said. "But how many books on the self-esteem shelf do you think people will be reading seventeen centuries from now?"

"All of them, I'm sure," Chris joked. "Especially the ones with the really nice fake smiles."

Gil chuckled and shook his head. "The self-esteem books try to make you feel better by avoiding sin. They miss it by a long shot. The greater your acknowledgment of your sinfulness, the greater your appreciation of God's grace."

"You know, who needs to go to church? I haven't even had breakfast yet, and you've already preached a sermon!"

"Bishop Augustine's preaching today, not me." Gil chuckled again, then pointed to the food. "Ready to eat?"

"Absolutely," Chris said.

"How about I quote one of my favorite prayers from *Confessions*?"

"Fine by me."

Gil put his hand on top of Chris's, closed his eyes, and quoted Augustine from memory. "Lord, You called and cried out loud and shattered our deafness. You were radiant and resplendent. You put to flight our blindness. You were fragrant, and we drew in our breath and now pant after You. We tasted You, and we feel nothing but hunger and thirst for You. You touched us, and we are set on fire to attain the peace which is Yours. Amen."

Gil looked down at the plate in front of him and smiled. "Thanks for breakfast, Chris."

"You're very welcome."

They ate in silence for a few minutes. Chris figured Gil was still thinking about Augustine, and when he spoke next, the thought was confirmed.

"Nothing like drinking from the deep wells of those who have gone before us. It's nice to think that the same God who conquered and won my heart so many years ago has been wooing people for thousands of years."

"I was just a kid," Chris said. "My conversion wasn't quite as dramatic as Augustine's. Or yours."

"Every conversion is dramatic," Gil said in his stately southern manner.

The two ate voraciously, the silence interrupted only by the clinking of their forks on the plate. When Chris finished, he sat back in his chair and breathed deeply, thinking about the faith he'd had as a child and about how that seemed to be changing.

"I'm glad you're here," Gil said. "I've been looking forward to catching up with you. We haven't had a good talk in a long while. Too long."

"Me too," Chris said, hiding his sadness from thinking about how that probably wasn't the only reason Gil was looking forward to the visit. His grandfather was clearly lonely.

Chris looked around the kitchen. Everything was simplified. The counters were clean where once they had been cluttered with spices and cooking supplies. No need for that bulky recipe book stuffed with notebook paper that had guided Grandma's hands as she labored over family feasts. The table was against the wall, a handful of framed family photos leaning backward against their stands on the tabletop. A couple of faded flower arrangements from the funeral were still standing in the corner.

The two sat silently in the kitchen for a moment. The stillness crept over Chris like the shadow of a cloud that harbors a rainstorm. Grandma was gone, and his grandfather seemed like a shadow of his former self, moving about much more haltingly and slowly than he had before the stroke.

"Why don't we move to the front room?" Gil said into the silence.

CHRIS LOVED A FIRE IN THE FIREPLACE, and he knew his grandfather did too. So he went to work at the vast stone hearth, with its stack of logs nearby. Soon flames and sparks were flying up the chimney.

Coming back to sit near his grandfather's recliner, Chris noticed a book on the table. "What are you reading there?" He didn't wait for Gil to answer. Instead, he picked it up himself. The title surprised him: *In Defense of Proselytism.* "Some light reading for the morning, huh?"

"It's an older book on evangelism," Gil said.

"Reading up on how you can proselytize me, huh?" Chris said.

Gil seemed taken aback. "I wouldn't have thought that would be necessary."

Chris suddenly felt he'd revealed too much. His face reddened. Up until now, Gil must have been thinking that Chris was merely struggling with some questions, not teetering on the edge of total unbelief.

"No," Gil continued. "I was revisiting some notes from it, in light of our talk last night."

"We didn't talk about evangelism," Chris said.

"But we were talking about the new church you're helping. And why you wanted to study theology. And Christianity compared to other religions. You must admit, evangelism is related to all that, especially if Christianity is more than ethics."

Chris put the book on the table with the cover facedown. "I don't see what that has to do with proselytizing people."

"Well, if Christianity isn't just about being a nice person, if it's about news—news about what God has done through Jesus Christ—then that message is vitally important. Eternal life hangs in the balance." Gil's tone was serious.

"Listen, Gramps, can I shoot straight with you?" Chris cleared his throat.

"Always."

"One of the reasons I stepped back from the new church is…well, frankly I'm uncomfortable with the idea of evangelizing someone." There. He'd said it. Now he waited for his granddad's reaction.

"Welcome to the club," Gil said.

"You're uncomfortable with it too?"

Gil shook his head as though he were embarrassed. "You'd best not think of me as an expert on the subject. I've always felt like my attempts to share my faith were feeble at best. Whenever I share the gospel, I feel like a clumsy kid handling a stick of dynamite. Maybe that's God teaching me a lesson. That the power's in the message, not the messenger. Good thing."

Chris loved his granddad's humility, and somehow it comforted him to know Gil felt inadequate as well. But he quickly realized they were talking about two different things. "That's not what I meant, Gramps. I'm not uncomfortable with the *act* of evangelism. It's the whole idea of it."

"Okay. Tell me more," Gil said.

"I'm not scared to talk to people about Christianity or about my church or about religious studies or about God in general. But I can't stomach the idea of pressing someone, trying to get him or her to come to my way of thinking."

Chris took a deep breath. He wondered how his grandfather would react. "I don't want to disrespect you, Gramps. You've done great work in your life." Should he tell him about the box of sermons he'd found? Ask about Katy? Not yet. "I'm sure you've got some strong opinions on this. You believe in evangelism and you've lived it out. But I don't have the same conviction."

Gil nodded his head slowly.

Chris went on. "Just a couple of weeks ago, I was talking to a friend of mine. She's Buddhist. We had some classes together, and we were standing next to each other in line at graduation. We were talking about our future plans. I mentioned that I was looking at some graduate programs in religious studies. That led to a few questions about Christianity. I answered her as best I knew how, but I didn't try to convince her to become a Christian."

"Why not?" Gil asked.

"For starters, I'm not the model Christian right now."

"Well, who is?"

"I don't mean *perfect* Christian. I mean *authentic* Christian."

"Well, who is totally authentic?"

"Okay, okay. Would you cut it out?" Chris loved the way his granddad leveled the playing field so that no one could claim a superior moral position. But for once Chris wanted to be the bad, doubt-filled, almost-apostate Christian without Gil's graciousness getting in the way. "Let me put it this way, then. I didn't feel comfortable evangelizing because I didn't want to come across like I think my religion is better than hers."

"And?" Gil said.

"And…well, I don't want to come across that way."

"You should realize something. Even if you didn't press her to become a Christian, you still gave her the impression that your faith—whatever faith you have—is better than hers."

"I'm not sure I follow you."

"You're a Christian—a follower of Christ," Gil said. "At least in name, and I hope in your heart." Chris sensed Gil's pastoral concern in his tone of voice, but that didn't stop his granddad from appealing to Chris's intellect. "That means you think Christianity is superior to other religions. And she's a Buddhist. That means she thinks Buddhism is superior."

"But she never said anything like that. And she doesn't come across that way," Chris said.

"Does she have to?" Gil said. "Listen, I think it's great that both of you are courteous and civil to each other. Lord knows we need more civility in this day and age. But make no mistake. Both of you think you're right, and both of you think the other is wrong."

"You're putting words in our mouths. That's exactly what we *didn't* say."

"Then you didn't admit the very thing that was most obvious." Gil shifted in his chair and leaned away from the table. "Let me ask you a question. If you don't think following Christ is better than the teachings of Buddhism, then why are you a Christian?"

"I grew up a Christian."

"Bad answer," Gil said. "Let me ask it the other way around. If your friend doesn't think Buddhism is better than Christianity, then why is she Buddhist?"

"I see what you're saying. The fact that you've chosen one religion over another means you must think it is better than the other."

"Precisely. If you don't think your religion is best, why not convert to whatever religion *is* best?"

"So let me get this straight. You're saying it's okay to believe that Christianity is superior?" Chris couldn't imagine his granddad would recommend anyone walking around, nose in the air.

"There's a difference between believing your religion is superior and having a superior attitude. Those are two different things."

"They sound pretty close to me." Chris slid the proselytism book toward Gil. "The minute you think your faith is better than someone else's, you start down the path of having a superior attitude."

"Sometimes that *is* the case," Gil said. "What's the alternative, then?"

Chris knew Gil was setting him up, so he gave it his best shot. What would Dr. Coleman say? He knew. "What if we said no religion is superior? What if we said all religions are on equal footing? That would keep people from having an attitude of superiority."

"You think so?" Gil said. Suddenly Chris wasn't so sure.

"Why wouldn't it?"

"That's a mighty big statement, if you ask me. To say no religion is better than another. To say all religions are equal. You know, that's a belief too. And I bet whoever says something like that probably believes that idea is better than yours or mine."

"I'm confused."

"My point is this: You don't lose the attitude of superiority by saying no religion is superior. You get even *more* reason to feel superior. Now you're standing over against *all* the religions of the world, saying none is better than another."

Chris chewed on that for a few moments. Gil had become animated. He'd drawn out the "all" when talking about the religions of the world, and he'd even used some hand gestures (with his right hand, of course). Still, Chris wasn't satisfied. "I think it's more openminded to leave room for different views of truth."

"Don't you find it just a wee bit prejudiced to say that we're the only ones who've figured out all religions are the same? All the while, there are poor, mindless Christians or Muslims or Buddhists or Hindus across the world still groping around in the dark. Poor souls. They think their religions are better." Gil winked at Chris.

"So, what are you saying? That there's no way around it? Okay, then. Maybe I do think Christianity is better. But that still doesn't sit well with me."

"That's because you're thinking of following Christ as if it's a preference. Like having a favorite color or something. Trying to push your favorite color on someone else would make anyone uncomfortable. But at the end of the day, we don't believe the gospel because it's helpful. Or because it's prettier. Or because it's our upbringing. We believe the gospel because it's *true*. Not just a preference but true. Truth about the way the world works."

"You may be right, but we could use better PR. We look bad

when we pressure people into becoming Christians. There's got to be a way to invite people to the Christian faith without proselytizing them."

"I heard that from lots of folks when I was a pastor," Gil said.

"What did you tell them?"

"Same thing I'm going to say to you. You claim to be a follower of King Jesus. So what do you do with the King's final instructions? 'Go and make disciples of all nations.'"

Chris had a feeling Gil wasn't finished yet. So he didn't answer. Instead, he got up to add a log to the fire and listened to Gil.

"What do you do with Jesus's prediction that the world would hate those who follow Him? What do you do with Jesus saying His disciples would be fishers of men?"

Chris stayed quiet.

"Not trying to clobber you with questions, Chris." Gil took off his glasses and rubbed his forehead. "Help me out here," he said. "Explain to me how someone can follow Jesus and disregard what He said."

Chris felt himself getting red, but it all seemed justified, especially since he'd practically just spelled out the seriousness of his spiritual crisis. Nevertheless, Chris decided to defend himself.

"Well, you and the Christians like you can go on with your little tracts and evangelistic crusades and your door-to-door knocking," Chris said. "But I've got news for you—it doesn't look good."

"How it looks is not the point." Gil put his glasses back on. "The question I'm asking you is, Can someone be a follower of Jesus Christ and not ever make disciples?" Gil's words hung in the air for a few moments. Chris had never considered this before.

"People who proselytize are arrogant."

"We don't proselytize," Gil said. "We evangelize. The book is mistitled."

"What's the difference?" Chris asked.

"Proselytism is about getting someone to change from one religion to another. Evangelism is proclaiming the evangel—the gospel. It's an announcement."

"Yeah, but evangelism is about changing from one religion to another too, right?"

"Evangelism is making a statement about the way the world is," Gil said. "Then you call people to bring their lives in line with that reality."

"Why not leave well enough alone? Let people think what they want? It still seems arrogant."

"Frankly, I think it's more arrogant to be against evangelism."

"Why is that?"

"Whoever says we should just keep our faith to ourselves and not evangelize—they're really saying we ought to follow *their* instructions and not King Jesus. *That* is the height of arrogance, in my mind. Trying to be over Him."

"So I guess the lesson for the day is, to be a good Christian means you just grit your teeth and do evangelism because Jesus said so," Chris said.

"No way," Gil said.

"But that's exactly what you're saying. No matter how uncomfortable you feel about it, you've got to do it anyway."

"Not at all. People rarely fail to evangelize because of their intellectual questions. Failure to evangelize is almost always a worship problem. It's not that we don't know what we ought to be doing. We do. We're just not doing it. That's a sign that we're not overflowing with worship. Whenever you are completely taken with something or someone, you can't help but talk about it. Kind of like how you talked about Ashley to me last spring. Love can't stop talking about the beloved. Fix the worship problem, and evangelism starts coming naturally."

CHRIS SUDDENLY HEARD MUSIC playing from somewhere. "Is that 'Joy to the World'?"

"Ah! My ringtone," Gil said. Chris was amazed his granddad knew what a ringtone was. Then again, he was into e-books.

"Where is your phone?"

Gil was about to stand up, when Chris hopped up first. "No, no. Stay there in your chair. I'll follow the sound of it." He stuck his head into the hallway and tried to discern what part of the house it was coming from.

"It should be in my room on my nightstand," Gil said.

Chris dashed into the bedroom, found the phone, and pressed Talk just before the song stopped.

"Hello?"

"Mr. Walker?" the voice on the other end of the line said.

"No, this is his grandson."

"Oh, hi! This is Katherine Reed. I'm the nurse who helps your granddad with his physical therapy."

Chris was back in the front room with his hand over the speaker. "It's your nurse," he whispered.

The woman on the phone continued. "I don't think I'm going to be able to make it this afternoon as we planned. The roads are still pretty bad out my way. Can you tell Gil I'm sorry? He should be able to do the exercises himself, as long as he has you to help him."

"I'll tell him," Chris said.

"All right, then. Happy New Year!"

"Same to you." Chris turned off the phone and handed it to Gil. "It was your nurse. She can't make it."

"Too bad you did all that hard work shoveling the drive last night," Gil said.

"Maybe the two of us will get out tomorrow. The ice doesn't stand a chance against that sun. She also said I could help you do the exercises." Chris wasn't sure how his grandpa would respond to his offer. After all, he was fiercely independent. Having his grandson help him do rehabilitation exercises probably wasn't one of his New Year's resolutions.

Gil hesitated, then nodded. "Well, I guess so. Let's go into my bedroom, and I'll show you what we need to do."

"We haven't finished our discussion yet," Chris said. "I'm not through protesting."

"Bring it on!" Gil said with a smile, standing up at the table. He grabbed his cane and hobbled across the hall.

Gil's insides had been in a knot ever since Chris had volunteered to help him with his physical therapy. It was bad enough to need a nurse every day. Her visits were a daily reminder that he was feeble—a long way from full recovery.

Gil sat down on his bed and asked Chris to move the chair closer to him. The room was dimly lit by the lamp on Gil's nightstand. "Pull those curtains back, will you?"

Chris opened the curtains and sunlight flooded the room. The glare from the snow and ice made the room so bright that Chris had to shield his eyes. The little light in the corner became redundant, so Gil reached over and turned it off.

"If you're okay talking about it, can you tell me what happened the day you had the stroke?" Chris asked.

"I was in the other bedroom going through Frances's stuff. And all of a sudden, my arm started to tingle and then went numb. Then my vision got blurry, like my eyes weren't working together. I knew something was wrong. So I got up to walk into the other room and call Ruth."

"You didn't make it, did you?" Chris said.

"The room was spinning. I got dizzy. I couldn't keep my balance. I knew if I tried to keep walking, I'd fall and break something. So I just laid down on the floor in the front room and started praying."

"That must've been scary."

"It was." Gil closed his eyes.

"How long were you by yourself?" Chris asked. Gil could tell Chris was bothered by the thought of him lying helpless on the floor.

"Just a few minutes. Ruth was already on her way over here for something else. She came in, called an ambulance, and helped me get over to the couch. My speech was slurred, but I was still able to talk."

"That's good."

"It'll take more than a stroke to shut me up," Gil said. He saw that Chris was deep in thought. "Come on, now," he said, patting him on the back. "Lighten up."

"All right," Chris said, shifting gears. "Now you're going to have to tell me what these exercises are that you're doing. I'm not a nurse, and I don't have a clue."

"Why don't we just skip 'em today?" Gil said. He wasn't in the mood.

"Oh no you don't," Chris said. "The nurse wouldn't have told me to help you if she didn't think you needed them."

Gil grunted.

"And since tomorrow is New Year's, you'd be going two full days without help if we don't do something now. So you just tell me what the exercises are, and I'll help you do them."

"All righty," Gil said, trying to cheer himself up. He dreaded the idea of his grandson seeing his weakness on full display. The exercises were helpful, but they demanded full disclosure of how hard Gil found it to do simple tasks.

"Let's start with the hand and fingers, then," he told Chris. "Hand me the little bed desk there." On the floor was a wooden platter that looked like a tray used in a hospital to serve meals to patients. Gil moved around in the bed and put his hands on the tray table.

"Fingers first?" Chris said.

"Okay." Gil put his left hand on the table and breathed deeply. "I'm going to raise and lower each finger ten times. Can you count for me?"

"Got it," Chris said.

Gil's index finger went up and down easy enough. The next finger was harder. By the time he got to his third finger, he was sweating. He could barely lift the finger off the table. Did Chris see how hard this was for him? Was there any way to hide it? *Dear old granddad lecturing on theology can barely lift his pinkie.*

"You're doing good, Gramps," Chris said.

After a few more minutes of finger exercises, they moved on to hand work. "Bring over that box," Gil told Chris. Gil worked on picking up and squeezing, in turn, a tennis ball, a pad of Post-it notes, a little measuring cup, a binder clip, a pencil, and a paper clip. As he moved from the larger objects to the smaller ones, they got harder and harder to pick up.

"A few weeks ago I couldn't do this at all," Gil said. Yes, he was making progress. Soon he would have the mobility of a toddler. *Forgive me, Lord,* he thought. *I have no right to complain.*

"Great job," Chris said.

"Picking up a paper clip doesn't deserve a medal."

"You're making progress, though."

"Okay, now for the balance exercises. I won't need help with these." Chris took the tray table away and helped Gil lie on the floor. Right away, Gil started his routine, bending his knees so that his feet were flat on the floor, then moving his knees gently from side to side.

"Forgive me for looking straight up at the ceiling and not at you while I do this. You're supposed to coordinate your vision and movement to help strengthen your balance. Or something like that," he said.

Gil wasn't tired, but it wearied him to think of Chris seeing him this way. Better to get back into some rich conversation, where his strengths would be on display. "If you want to do these exercises with me, you can get out the box of weights under the bed. That's next on my list."

Now this must be a sight, Gil thought. *An old man on the floor doing leg stretches and posture exercises, next to his grandson sitting up doing some piddling weightlifting. The meek will inherit the earth.*

Chris seemed to recognize Gil's discomfort, and he changed the subject, mercifully.

"I SEE WHERE YOU'RE COMING from, Gramps, on the whole evangelism thing. But it doesn't make evangelism any easier."

"Christianity is many things, but easy is not one of them," Gil said, glad they were talking again.

"Christianity isn't popular either," Chris added.

"Especially when we evangelize," said Gil. "People may think we Christians are intolerant, exclusivist, and arrogant. But don't ever let go of the fact that Christianity is radically *in*clusive."

"Inclusive?"

"Of course. King Jesus commissioned us to call *all* people *everywhere* to repentance and faith. People from every tongue, tribe, and nation. People of every color, ethnicity, and background. People from every religion. We evangelize because the call to salvation is *in*clusive."

"So you're saying I should call my Buddhist friend to trust in Christ because I'm *in*clusive?" Chris's smirk looked like a younger variation of Gil's.

"That's right," Gil said softly. "At the end of the day, the narrow-minded, prejudiced Christian is the one who looks at a Buddhist friend and stays quiet about Jesus. When you stay silent, what you're saying is, 'Jesus isn't for me.'"

"But whenever you tell someone they should become a Christian, you're saying that whatever they already believe is deficient somehow. They're inferior for not believing what you do."

"You're right on the first statement but wrong on the second."

"Okay. So…"

"You're right that evangelism means whatever the other person believes is deficient. But you're wrong that it means *they* are inferior for not believing the way you do."

"Don't they go together?"

"You tell me. Do you believe that no religious belief has any deficiency? That every religion is equally good? Equally valid—just different?"

"I didn't say they're all the same."

"Well, it sure sounded that way last night. But never mind. I'm glad you see they're different. To say all religions are the same is disrespectful. Buddhists know they're not Christians. Christians know they're not Muslims. Never downplay the differences between these faiths."

"Sometimes it wouldn't hurt us to be a little more like other religions," Chris put in. "After all, Christianity produced the Crusades, the Inquisition. Lots of Christians supported slavery. People around here, even in your church, wanted segregation."

The words stung. There was a tone in Chris's voice that seemed to make Lewisville out to be an ignorant, backwater town full of racists. Gil wondered if he should give some of his own personal history of that time and how his church had responded. He groaned, partly from the exercises, partly from the memory. *Lost church members over how I handled that.* He decided to let it go.

"Oh, we've got our dark moments in history, that's for sure," Gil said. "But we fess up. Not to mention we can offer a good explanation for them."

"There is *no* justification for all that."

"Not a justification, mind you," Gil said. "But an explanation, yes."

"And what is that?"

"Sin, of course. Human wickedness. Evil. Even when we have the best intentions, we muddle things up."

Gil could tell that Chris didn't like that answer. Too simplistic? *When in doubt, keep talking.*

"We sure look like a hopeless lot, don't we? A bungling bunch of believers. It's only through grace we've made it two thousand years. Heresy threatening us from inside the walls, persecution from outside. Compromise with powers and principalities. Damaging our witness. Diluting our influence. And still we venture on, this disheveled bride, this disabled body, this unruly flock. Christ hasn't given up on us yet."

"That's a cop-out," Chris said.

Gil loved it when Chris got feisty. Gil could wax eloquently about lots of things, but Chris had a knack for peeling back the layers and getting to the nub of what he didn't like. *A lot like his granddad, I must say.*

"You're taking all those times of Christian failure and chalking them up to sin. That doesn't do justice to just how bad things were, does it?"

"I am not justifying the Christians in the past, just as I don't try and justify my own personal sins in the present. There's only one kind of justification that matters, and it's not brought about by ourselves. That's why no Christian who truly understands grace can feel superior to anyone else. Grace shatters any sense of superiority."

"But you're putting off those sins and failures. You're just blaming human weakness for them. Christians have done terrible things, and you are minimizing them. The same way you minimized what Dad did."

The words pierced the air and changed the atmosphere. Gil froze in position, trying to hide his hurt. The idea that he would ever seek to justify or excuse his son's behavior made his whole body tighten up. But he held his tongue. He would not defend his honor; nor would he continue down that road. He hoisted himself up into a sitting position with his back against the bed.

"I-I'm sorry, Gramps," Chris said. He wouldn't look him in the eye. But that didn't stop Gil from looking at his grandson.

After a deep breath, Gil responded. "Chris, I love your sense of justice. You see the failures of people in the past so clearly. You're right to be angry at your dad. Angry at me too."

"I'm not angry at you," Chris said, shaking his head. "I was just spouting off."

Gil sat there in the heaviness of the moment for a bit before continuing. "The truth is, you're like a kid in a tree who is sawing off the branch he's sitting on." Gil grinned.

"What do you mean by that?" Now Chris looked a little offended.

"You want to criticize Christian hypocrisy by cutting off the branch of Christian morality. Here's the big question. Where do you get the right to judge Christians in the past? Where do you get the right to judge people like your dad?"

"I am not judging."

"But you are. And that sense of righteous indignation—I love that about you—it comes from your Christian faith. Your ideals are rooted in a Christian view of how the world should run. And when you see Christians failing to live up to those ideals, you get upset."

"So you're saying my criticism of the church is Christian criticism?"

"Yes. Christianity gives you the ideal—what the church should be. It also gives you the doctrine that explains the reality—original sin. That's why the church fails to be all it should be. Once you hold together the ideals of Christianity with the reality of human fallenness...well, let me just say that your critique of Christian history is based on a Christian view of justice. Sounds to me like you're establishing the truth of Christianity at the same time you're critiquing it."

"Nice try," said Chris. "But maybe the Achilles' heel of Christianity is that no one has ever lived up to it. What if hypocrisy is the sign that the whole thing is a sham?"

"I think it's time for me to lift some weights." Gil smiled and changed the subject. He was weary from the talk and felt emotionally drained from Chris's earlier accusation. He reached his arm out and had Chris help him stand to his feet.

GIL STARTED LIFTING THE SMALL weights with his left arm, doing his best to maintain a firm grip. After a couple of minutes, the difficulty was hard to hide. Gil didn't want Chris to see him give up too soon.

"Am I supposed to massage your leg or something?" Chris said.

Gil groaned inside. *This kid is too smart.*

"Nothing we've done so far you couldn't have done on your own.

So unless your nurse comes over here every day just to be your cheer-leader, I'm guessing she does something else."

"Nothing gets past you, does it?" Gil grinned. "My joints around the knee ache, and part of the way she keeps me mobile is by massaging them."

"So, how do I do it?"

"Now, now. You're not a specialist."

"It can't be that hard, can it? She told me to help."

"I don't know how to explain what she does." Gil thought he could avoid the massage. As good as it made him feel, he didn't want to go through the humiliation of having his grandson see how thin and frail his leg was. As long as he was in sweatpants, he could mask his disability.

"I'll just call her, then." Chris hopped up and left the room.

Chris's voice carried down the hall. A minute or two later, he returned with a pencil behind his ear and a notepad filled with instructions. "Okay. I think I got this down," he said.

"Let's hope so," Gil said, trying to not let his lack of enthusiasm show too strongly.

"Roll up your pant leg," Chris said. He was barking out instructions as if he were a pro.

"Don't get too cocky there," Gil said.

Chris grinned at him.

Gil rolled up the sweatpants—both legs.

"I don't need to do both, do I?" asked Chris.

"The goal is to get the left leg in the same shape as the right one. So that both are equally strong again." Truth was, Gil was embarrassed by the weakness on display in his left leg. He wanted Chris to see the right one so he wouldn't think he had wasted away completely.

Chris didn't appear to be surprised by either leg, which made Gil wonder if maybe he was just being too self-conscious.

"I want to ask you about something I was thinking last night," Chris said as he was starting the massage.

"Shouldn't you concentrate right now on following those instructions?"

"I can multitask."

Not reassuring. "Okay," Gil said. "It's just my joints we're dealing with."

Chris didn't say anything more. Gil was quiet too and let Chris concentrate on following the instructions on the notepad. He was doing a pretty good job. He wasn't as firm as the nurse, but that's probably because he was afraid of hurting his granddad or doing damage to the bones and nerves.

A few minutes later, they were done. There were some other exercises and massage therapy in the routine, but if the nurse hadn't told Chris about them, then Gil sure wasn't going to publicize them.

"Thank you, Chris." He was sincere. Though the situation didn't agree with him, he was grateful for Chris's willingness to help.

"That's what I'm here for," Chris said.

Gil rolled his sweatpants back down, took his cane from the bedside, and made his way to the recliner in the room. Chris sat down on the side of the bed. Both of them looked out the window. "Snow is finally melting," Chris said. Gil could hear the sound of water splashing out of the gutters alongside the house. The brittle ice was giving way to the goodness of the sun's warmth.

THE ROOM WAS QUIET as the two admired the peaceful hillside covered in snow just outside the window. A moment later, a bang rattled the windowpane and caused both Chris and Gil to jump.

"What was that?" Chris said. He ran to the window.

"It was a bird," Gil said.

"A bird?"

"Happens every now and then. The window is so big that when the sun is out, the birds sometimes get confused. And here they come, smashing into the window."

"Are you sure it was a bird?"

"Let's go see."

Chris helped Gil get up, and the two of them walked to the door that led from the bedroom out onto the wraparound porch. The sun was shining directly on them, which helped them not feel the cold air as strongly. The two of them stood on the porch and looked over to the ground outside the big window. Sure enough, there was a bird, fluttering a wing and writhing painfully on the ground.

"It's a chickadee," Gil said. "The chickadees and cardinals hang around during the winter."

"Can we help it?"

"Depends on how hard it banged its head," Gil said. "Sometimes they're just dazed. But usually they're dead. Poor little things."

Chris ran back inside, mumbling something about a box. He was on a rescue mission to keep that little bird from dying. Gil watched the bird. Within a minute, it had stopped moving completely. By the time Chris got back, Gil knew it was too late.

Chris pulled off his socks and stepped off the porch in his bare feet, hopping around in the ice and snow, his mind preoccupied with the bird. He scooped it up in his hands and put it in the box. In a flash, he was back on the porch, drying his feet on the rug outside Gil's bedroom door.

They made their way back inside the bedroom. There was no sound or movement from the bird in the box. Chris stroked the large white area on its breast. Gil was impressed by his sense of compassion for the bird.

"It's so random, really. Why this bird? Why today?" Chris seemed to be talking to himself. But then he looked up at Gil. "Ever wonder if maybe there isn't any big purpose to life?"

Gil smiled. "I don't think this bird hit the window so we could have a conversation about the meaning of life," he said.

As if on cue, the bird's wings fluttered suddenly and the chickadee burst out of the box and into the room. It soared up to the ceiling and then to the window, pecking at it as if it were strong enough to make it give way. "Quick, shut the doors!" Gil cried.

Chris darted to the bedroom door and closed it, to make sure the bird didn't get into the hall and the rest of the house. Gil had already made his way to the bathroom door, surprising himself by his speed. It was the first time he'd moved that quickly since before the stroke.

With the bird contained, fluttering up into the corners of the room and constantly going back to the window, Gil grabbed a magazine from his nightstand.

Chris opened the door that went onto the porch and tried to call the bird. "Here, birdie! Here!"

"It's not a puppy dog," Gil said. "It's not going to come to you if you call it. You'll have to shoo it out."

"But how?" The bird was making constant attempts to get out through the window. Although banging its head on the outside of the window hadn't killed it, it might kill itself by banging its head from the inside.

"It knows it needs to get outside but doesn't know the way," Gil said.

"Yeah, I figured that out."

"No need to get smart with me." Gil grinned at Chris, flipped open the magazine, and said to the bird, "This is for your own good." Then he smacked the crazy chickadee firmly from the side and swooshed it toward the door. Chris ducked when he saw the bird coming at him, and within moments it had flown outside and out of sight.

Unfortunately, Gil's attempt to sweep the bird outside had caused him to turn around suddenly and stumble. Gil saw Chris lunging toward him, hoping to catch him, but it was too late. He dropped the magazine and crumpled onto the floor next to the couch.

"Are you okay?" Chris was hovering over him, pulling and yanking at his shoulders and back.

"I think so," Gil said, breathing heavily. *No sharp pains, thank God.* One of his biggest worries was that he would break a hip or some other bone in a moment of stupidity. That's why he'd been extra careful since the stroke.

Chris helped Gil up onto the couch by the window. "I'm okay… I'm okay…" He sought to reassure Chris and himself.

"Are you sure, Gramps?"

Gil opened his eyes and looked straight at Chris. "I'm fine. Really. Just let me be." He realized he must sound impatient and frustrated. But he didn't feel like apologizing. Had Chris left well enough alone, the bird would have been fine and Gil wouldn't have nearly put himself in the hospital.

"I think I've had enough activity for one morning," he said. "I'm going to lie down a bit, if that's okay with you."

"Sure thing," Chris said.

Chris left the room and closed the door. Gil walked back to his bed and stretched out on top of the blankets, his heart beating fiercely. *Close one.*

Gil's oak roll-top desk held a certain allure for Chris. It was the one thing in the front room that caught Chris's eye every time he walked in. The shelves above the desk were filled with books, most of which looked old. These were the best of the best, the books Gil had saved when he'd donated his extensive library to a Bible college. That meant these books were either excellent, in Gil's opinion, or meant a lot to him personally.

The spines of many of these books announced familiar names. Chesterton. Lewis. Spurgeon. Wesley. Edwards. A plaque next to a bookend featured a quote from Charles Spurgeon: "The old, old gospel is the newest thing in the world; in its very essence it is for ever good news."

Since Gil was resting, Chris decided to lose himself in some of the old books. He sprawled out on the sofa and lost track of time as he dipped into Gil's collection of classics.

After a couple of hours, Chris suddenly noticed the house was still quiet. He glanced at the clock and saw that it was well past lunchtime. He went into the kitchen, pulled out the sandwich platter, and set the table. There wasn't much to prepare.

While he waited for his grandfather to appear, he spent some time looking at pictures of Ashley on his phone. He missed her. Though they had been apart for months now, Chris still felt miserable when he thought of her. Unlike other girlfriends he'd broken up with, Ashley wasn't vacating his heart. If she was going to leave it, he was going to have to push her out. But a big part of him wanted her to stay forever.

He put down the phone and started reading a copy of the local paper he found on the table. It was already a couple of days old. No matter. Chris found Lewisville news fascinating, primarily because the smallness of the town meant the reporters had to work overtime finding stories to report. Chris was so engrossed in the local news tidbits that he didn't realize Gil had appeared in the kitchen doorway until his grandfather asked, "Hungry?"

"Oh. Not really, but let's eat anyway," Chris said. "Did you get some rest?"

"I'm feeling better." Gil took a seat at the table.

The two prayed and ate their sandwiches quickly, talking only about some of the things Chris had seen in the newspaper. It seemed to Chris like they were both trying to put the awkward morning out of their minds. Eventually, Chris felt that he should own up to his rummaging around in the closet during the middle of the night.

"Gramps, I couldn't sleep last night. So I did a little exploring. I hope you don't mind."

"Man was made to explore," Gil said. "What did you find stowed away in this old house?"

"I found all your sermons," Chris said.

Gil nodded his head, evidently pleased that Chris had come across them. "My life's work," he said, then added quietly, "now stuffed into one box and stored in a closet."

There was a tinge of sadness to that comment, making Chris eager to change the subject. "I found a sermon that was interesting. I want to hear the story behind it."

"Thank you for the compliment. You obviously have forgotten my age and think my memory is better than it is."

"No, really. I think you'll remember this one," Chris said. "Just a minute." He jumped up from the table, ran upstairs, and grabbed the sermon outline on the nightstand in Aunt Ruth's old room. Within seconds, he was back at the table in the kitchen.

"Training for the Olympics, are you now?" Gil said.

Chris handed over the sermon outline. Gil pushed his eyeglasses down his nose and peered at the messy handwriting. Chris began telling him everything he knew. "I saw there was a Katy mentioned a few times. It was a sermon you did for the teenagers. A lot of stuff about forgiveness and rejecting popularity for Jesus. I looked up the church directories and found a Katy Baisley. I assume it's the same girl. She's in 1975 and 1978, but not in 1980, and her family isn't in 1985."

Gil looked up from the sermon outline and extended his hand to Chris. "Congratulations. You missed your calling. You ought to be a detective."

Chris laughed. "Come on, Gramps. Surely I've jarred your memory. You've got to know what it's all about."

"Oh, I didn't need your summary to remember this. A sermon like this stays with you."

"Well, then? Who was Katy Baisley and what's her story?"

GIL PUT THE PIECE OF PAPER DOWN and pushed his glasses back up his nose. "We had a crisis in the church in the late 1970s," he said.

"And Katy was the cause?"

"As I was saying, we had a crisis in the church in the 1970s. It was mainly in the youth group. And those who were coming back from college. There were different winds blowing back then. The sexual revolution and all that. 'Free love' was happening in the 1960s across the country, but it takes about a decade or so for things to trickle down to the common folk in places like Lewisville."

Chris was already engaged in the story, to the point that he forgot the sandwich he was finishing. A bit of mayonnaise was dribbling down his chin. Gil made a motion to let him know, and Chris wiped his face with a napkin.

"Katy Baisley grew up in Lewisville. Her family attended our church. They tended to be a Sunday-morning-only type of family, but faithful in that. I baptized Katy." He paused, searching his memory. "I'm guessing it was when she was twelve or thirteen. A whole bunch of teenagers got baptized one summer after camp. But I don't remember exactly."

Gil continued. "Anyway, that's not the point of the story. When Katy got to be about fifteen, she got a little rebellious. Started sneaking out of her house at night and meeting a guy who had dropped out of high school. The two of them started sleeping together, and no one in her family knew about it."

"So let me guess," Chris said. "She got pregnant. There was an uproar in the church. She got kicked out, and that's why she's not in the directory ever again."

"Will you just hold your horses?" Gil said. "I take back what I said about you being a detective."

"She didn't get pregnant?"

"No. What she did was start telling of all her exploits to the other young ladies in the youth group. Come to find out, a lot of our young folks were buying into the lie of sex without consequences."

"So, how did you find out about all this?"

"Katy's parents found out. Caught her coming back in one night. They came to me directly, heartbroken, wondering what to do."

"How did you respond?"

"I started digging around for more information, and I realized we had a full-blown mutiny taking place in the youth group. On the surface everything was good. Nice-looking kids going on mission trips, going to camp, visiting the shut-ins, singing in the choir. But after I talked to a few of the youth—guys and gals—well, I realized something was up. There was a mood of rebellion against the morality of their parents, against Christian teaching in general. Word had gotten out about Katy's behavior. One of those situations where everyone says, 'I didn't tell a soul, and they all promised to keep it a secret!' It was the talk of the town."

"Not a good situation."

"We had to do something. The testimony of the church was at stake. More than that, the representation of King Jesus Himself was at stake. We couldn't afford to not deal with the situation. We wanted Katy to be brought to repentance and the damage she'd done to be contained."

Gil stopped telling the story and munched on a few chips. "What would *you* have done?" he asked.

Chris was surprised to be in the hot seat. He shrugged and said, "I...well, I don't think I'm the best person to ask about this kind of thing. I don't know that I agree with what our churches say about sex and morals and all that."

Chris felt like he'd said something wrong, the way he'd felt earlier when challenging his granddad on evangelism. Then again, there was no sense hiding his doubts.

Gil was quiet for a moment. Then he began again. "Frances and I counseled Katy. She did repent. She actually became one of the strongest voices for purity in the youth group. The sermon outline you've got here was my first address to the youth group after the word got out. I was using Katy's story as an example. And I wanted to challenge the kids to go against the world. To be *against* the world for the good of the world."

"What happened to Katy? Why isn't she in the 1980 directory?"

"I reckon she was already in nursing school when we did the photos for that one. She would've been eighteen by then. She got married shortly after."

"Well, well," Chris said.

"It's funny that you'd ask about her, especially since you talked to her this morning."

What? Chris didn't understand. Then suddenly—*The nurse!* Chris was stunned. She'd said her name was Katherine Reed. *That* was Katy.

"Oh, don't look so surprised," Gil said. "The saying 'It's a small world' is doubly true when you live in a town like Lewisville."

Chris shook his head in disbelief. "I guess she's older now."

"She's a grandmother already."

Chris sat back in his chair, still surprised. "Wow."

"Tell me," Gil said. "What's this you said about having your own issues with Christian morality? Let's have at it!" He smiled and slapped Chris on the back.

Should they talk about this? Chris felt odd bringing up the subject.

"You feel weird talking about this with a man that's eighty years old, is that it?"

Chris didn't nod, but the way he pushed his lips to one side and opened his eyes wide said it all. "Not really...in general," he said, stumbling over the words. "You see, there's a situation. Well, really, I'm just not sure...you know the question of why is—"

"Slow down, son," Gil said. "Back that horse and carriage up a wee bit, will you? Start at the beginning."

CHRIS GOT QUIET. THIS WASN'T the kind of thing you jumped into. He had a specific friend in mind, but he decided it would be more comfortable to deal with hypothetical situations than with real people. "Okay. Let me put it this way. The Bible says we are to love all people."

"That's right."

"But the church isn't very loving when it comes to gay people," Chris said. He felt awkward bringing up homosexuality in the conversation, but Gil didn't seem fazed by it in the least. "The church takes a pretty unloving position, if you ask me."

"Why do you say that?" Gil asked.

"Let me ask you this," Chris said. "Would gays and lesbians be welcome at Third Baptist Church?"

Gil looked straight in Chris's eyes with an expression of surprise and sadness. "I'm surprised you'd even ask that kind of question, Chris. Don't you know me?"

Chris was confused. He wasn't sure if Gil was saying "Yes, homosexuals would be welcome" or "Of course not, how could you think such a thing?" There was a pained look on his grandfather's face.

Gil took off his glasses and sighed. "I have given my life to getting out a message that is for every person on this planet. I want everyone everywhere to hear the gospel. To be saved. To know King Jesus."

"You're not answering my question," Chris said.

"You know the folks at Third. Our arms are open to people from every background, every race, every ethnicity, every culture. Why, we lost a deacon and his family when I baptized a white man married to a black woman!"

"So the church would be open to gays?"

"We're a place for all kinds of sinners and people with all kinds of problems."

"Wait a second," Chris said. "You said, 'We're a place for all kinds of sinners.' So you do believe homosexuality is sinful, right?"

"Yes, of course. I believe the Bible." Gil didn't appear to be tracking with Chris's protest.

"But if we're Christians, and we're called to love all people, then how can we take the hard line on homosexuality? That's intolerant."

Gil put his elbows on the table and pushed his chair back on two legs. He tilted his head, smiled, and said, "Oh boy! You think the church's position on homosexuality is radical. What about everything else we believe about sex?"

"That being?"

"The teenage guy and girl in the backseat of a car. That's sin. Amber and Chad, who live two houses down from here—they're not married. That's sin too. What your dad did. Sin. The Bible's quite clear. Any sex outside of the marriage covenant is sinful."

"I hear you," Chris said. When he thought about the pain his father had caused through his philandering, it became momentarily easier to think about sexual sin being just plain wrong.

"King Jesus is a moral zealot when it comes to sex. He gets right to the heart of the matter. Remember Matthew 5? Every time you or I or anyone else even *lusts,* we're sinning."

"So you're saying we ought to be as radical as Jesus."

"I'm saying, once you understand King Jesus's teaching on sexuality, you see that all of us are sexual sinners. We're all sinful. That's why He came to die. He died to save lustful, self-centered, homosexual, heterosexual, whatever other kind of sexual sinners. And He came to transform us. Our hearts. Our minds. Our behavior."

Gil continued, "Now, because He died for me, I owe Him my all. And as a follower of King Jesus, I'm bound to what He says about sex and morality." Gil put the chair back down and pushed his plate with the sandwich crusts out of the way.

Chris immediately remembered an argument he'd heard. "But Jesus never condemned homosexuality."

"He didn't have to," Gil replied. "He went to the heart of the issue. Watch Him in the Sermon on the Mount. How He intensifies the commands against immoral behavior from the Old Testament."

"Intensifies?"

"Sure. King Jesus doesn't just condemn adultery, like the Ten Commandments do. He condemns even the lust that leads to adultery! You know why? Because He's offering us transformation. New hearts that will beat in step with His radical demands."

"But He chose not to condemn the woman caught in adultery."

"That's right. But then He told her to 'go, and sin no more.' He didn't *not* condemn her so she could continue living in sin. His declaration of 'no condemnation' changed her life so she could leave her life of sin."

Chris had other objections he wanted to get to. "Okay, let's leave Jesus for a minute."

"That's never a good idea," Gil said with a grin that showed he was only halfway teasing. He drank some orange juice.

"You know what I mean," Chris said. This conversation wasn't as awkward as he'd expected. But it was still rather unusual. "Who are you to condemn someone who doesn't have the same personal beliefs about sex?"

"Who am I?" Gil pointed to himself. "No one, really. It's not all that important what I think about these things."

"No?"

"No. This conversation is about King Jesus and what He says. I've got no right to condemn or judge anybody. That right belongs to the King. I'm just trying to follow Him faithfully. So, whatever *He* says about sex—that's what I choose to believe is the true and most loving way. I think His way is best for humans to flourish."

"Even if people everywhere else disagree with you?" Chris said. "Even if you're way out of the mainstream?"

"King Jesus has never been mainstream," Gil said. "You find a Jesus who fits into the mainstream, and I guarantee you haven't found the real Jesus."

"It's not popular nowadays to say that homosexuality is a sin. People aren't putting up with that anymore."

"People didn't like it much when John the Baptist called out the king for committing adultery either. Certain flaws were tolerated then. They're celebrated now. But remember this—a flaw is no less a flaw because it's fashionable."

"But isn't that judgmental? You're saying that gay people are flawed and sinful."

"I'm not singling out gay people. I'm pointing to Jesus. He's the answer to *all* sexual sinfulness. All of us are flawed and sinful."

Chris couldn't take it anymore. He had to bring up Chase. But it wouldn't be easy.

CHRIS CLEARED HIS THROAT. "I've got a friend who's gay."

"Chase?" Gil asked.

Chase was Chris's best friend growing up. The two lived in the same neighborhood and went to the same church. They'd been on mission trips together and had graduated from the same high school. Gil had met Chase more than once when the two boys were younger, but it was a mystery to Chris how Gil could have identified Chase as the friend he was talking about.

"How did you know?"

Gil tilted his head toward the picture of Chris's mother on the kitchen table.

"I should've known," Chris said, rolling his eyes. "Anyway, Chase tells me a few months ago that he's gay."

"What did you say?"

"I told him the Bible didn't go for that kind of thing. I didn't know what else to tell him."

"What did he say?"

"He started talking about how he was still a Christian. He couldn't believe I would judge him. That he'd like to stay friends with me, but I'd have to get behind him and support him for who he is." Chris remembered how horribly that conversation with Chase had ended. He wished he could rewind the discussion. If he were no longer a Christian, it would be so much easier. He could just affirm whatever decisions Chase made and never bring it up again.

Gil looked sad. There was a sense of heaviness on him that was emotional, not physical, for once. The heaviness spread to Chris, who suddenly felt a lump in his throat.

"I miss him, Gramps. He was my best friend." Chris felt as if he could cry. "What do you say? Can a Christian and a homosexual be friends?"

Gil was quiet for a moment and then quoted the lines from a hymn:

Beneath the shadow of the cross
The heavy-laden soul finds rest
I would esteem the world but dross
So I might be of Christ possessed.
Smile on me, gracious Lord.
Show thyself the friend of sinners now.

There was reverence in the air. It was as if Gil had been transformed into his pastor self from twenty years before, and he was in his study counseling a young man. Grandpa Gil was Pastor Gil in that moment.

"Chris, why would you ever think you can't be a friend to a sinner? Jesus is the mighty Friend of sinners to us. Why would we not be the friends of sinners?"

Chris nodded.

"You are sensing the tension every Christian feels. Love the sinner, hate the sin. Loving your neighbor without approving of everything your neighbor does," Gil said. "All of us are forced into that position one way or another—no matter the sin."

Gil continued, "When you think about it, that's the war we fight ourselves. We love ourselves—have no trouble with that at all—and yet, as Christians, we don't condone our own behavior half the time. Like Paul, we wrestle and realize what wretched people we are, before arriving at the throne of grace and saying, 'Thanks be to God through Jesus Christ our Lord.'"

"I can't judge anyone. I'm so far from perfect, Gramps. Everyone at the new church thinks I've got it all together. They think I'm rock solid in my beliefs. They think I'm going to be a leader. And I've got my own issues. I'm not sure what I believe all the time. I'm questioning everything. I've been drinking too much lately. I look at porn every now and then. I feel like such a hypocrite. I put out these ideals, and I don't even live up to them half the time."

Gil scooted his chair closer to Chris and put his arm around his shoulder. "This is the Christian life," he said. "It's war, Chris."

"But it's so hard."

"Indeed. I've been living for King Jesus for sixty years now, and the mountains are only steeper and the valleys are even deeper.

"Listen here," Gil said as he lifted Chris's chin. "There are only two ways to resolve the pressure you're feeling about being a hypocrite. You can do away with the ideal. Stop fighting your sin and abandon your faith. Or you can admit your failures. Strive in the power of the Holy Spirit and look to Jesus. Some people want to resolve hypocrisy by lowering the ideal. But instead, we ought to take the hand of Christ and move higher."

"That's not what Chase is going to do."

"I'm sorry to hear that."

"He's convinced he can go on living the way he's living and be a Christian. Like nothing has changed."

"That's not the case."

Chris looked Gil straight in the eyes. "Are you saying you can't be gay and Christian?"

"No," Gil said firmly. "I'm saying you can't be a Christian without repentance. All of us—you, me, Chase—every one of us is guilty of sin. But Christianity hinges on repentance. We have the Holy Spirit to convict us, we agree with God about our sin, and we turn from it and toward Jesus."

"So Chase isn't agreeing with God about his sin? Is that what you're saying?"

"It appears that way right now," Gil said. "But I want you to realize this conversation isn't really about homosexuality, or any other particular sin for that matter. It's about whether or not repentance is a must for the Christian life."

"If I ever told Chase that, he would think I'm attacking him personally." Chris shook his head. "It would be like I'm saying something is wrong with him."

"That's just the point," Gil said. "Look at what King Jesus says about sex and you'll quickly realize there's something wrong with all of us. Something wrong that can only be fixed by what Jesus did for us on the cross and in His resurrection."

"But he's still going to think I'm attacking him."

"That might be the case."

"He says he was born this way. That he's had these feelings for as long as he can remember."

"Don't discount his testimony about that," Gil said.

"So you agree it's not a choice?"

"Oh, he's making choices, all right. But to him it probably feels more complicated than that."

"He said he never woke up and decided he wanted to be this way."

"I'm sure that's true. No one ever woke up and decided, 'I want to have a bad temper.' Or 'I want to be addicted to pornography.' You don't always choose your temptations, but you do choose your behavior."

"He sees this as being the core of who he is, though. That's why he's come out with the label and is telling people he's gay. So now, if I question his behavior or his desires, he's going to feel as though I'm attacking the core of who he is."

"That's not your intention, though," Gil said.

"No, but that's the way he'll take it."

"Likely so."

"So tell me this. If a person is born with one sexual orientation or another, then how can it possibly be loving to blame someone for their attractions?"

"Let's back up a little there, Chris. We don't know about sexual attraction being innate and set from birth. True, you've got people saying they've had these attractions since they were kids. And yes, the Bible teaches that we're all bent toward sin. It may be that some have a propensity toward alcohol abuse or angry outbursts, while others have a propensity toward other sins. I don't know. I never want to say more than what the Bible says. Besides, even if that were the case, it's not hard to understand why people would see sexual desire as closer to the core of who they are."

"Well, Chase feels like that's how it is. So who am I to say he's wrong? I've got my own temptations and sins."

"Remember, we don't choose our temptations, but we do choose our behaviors. Chris, think about what we're saying about human beings if we define ourselves by whatever sexual urges we have. Is that all we are? Are we nothing more than our sexual temptations? Is that the defining thing about us?"

"What do you mean?"

"Let's say you get married," Gil said.

Chris immediately thought of Ashley, and his heart leaped and sunk at the same time.

"Now, when you get married," Gil went on, "you may find that you're still attracted to other women. Women you're *not* married to. Does this mean you ought to call yourself a polygamist?"

"Hope not," Chris said. He managed a smile.

"'Hope not'? Of course not! And would you consider me a bigot or hateful if I as a Christian pastor were to tell you *not* to act on those desires? If I were to say, 'Stay faithful to your wife'?"

"No." Again Chris thought of his father.

"Exactly. We are not defined by our temptations. We are defined by our redemption."

"But Chase says he has to be this way. Otherwise, he's not being true to who he is."

"That's because he sees his desires at the core of his being. But Jesus never says be true to yourself. Jesus says to be true—"

"To your future self," Chris finished the phrase for him. Gil looked surprised, so Chris reached down, picked up the sermon outline, and pointed out the phrase to him. "April 19, 1978, Gramps. You've been at this a long time."

"Indeed," said Gil with a tinge of weariness in his voice, as if the long years were catching up with him.

Chris got up and started collecting the dishes to take them to the sink and clean them. "It's going to get a lot harder to be a Christian who thinks this way."

"It's always hard to be a follower of Jesus."

"I mean, socially."

"You're right. Christians like me are certainly going to pay a social cost for holding the line on issues like this one."

Chris sighed. "Don't you think people have used this kind of talk to justify hate and bullying?"

"Some have," Gil said. "To their shame. A Christian ought to remember that every human being is made in God's image," Gil said. "But I'm also concerned that the traditional Christian perspective is about to be ruled out of bounds, as if holding to Jesus's view of sexuality is the same thing as hating other people. It's not. To differ is not to hate."

"So you say I ought to keep loving Chase but I shouldn't accept his behavior or choices."

"Yes."

"That's impossible. You can't love someone you don't affirm."

"Impossible? Well, I can tell you it's not." Gil paused and got quiet, as if he were deliberating whether he should say something. "I never stopped loving Stan."

"UNCLE STAN?" CHRIS'S EYES GOT BIG, and he turned around at the sink to look straight at his grandfather. "Your brother Stan?"

Gil nodded.

"Uncle Stan was—"

"Yes," Gil said. "It was whispered about around town. People didn't talk about stuff like that openly back then. But it was true. Stan confided in me when we were teenagers. Believe me, if you think it's hard to disagree so strongly with a friend, imagine it being your brother!"

"After he told me," Gil went on, "I couldn't help myself. I loved him even more. For years, I thought he would never repent. One night I remember Frances standing right over there at the sink doing the dishes as you're doing. And I said, 'It will take a miracle for Stan to get saved.' She looked at me and said, 'Of course it will. It always does.' She was right. Every conversion is a miracle, a supernatural work of the Holy Spirit."

"But wasn't Stan a member of your church?"

"By the time you knew him, yes. He was a deacon, actually."

Chris put his hand to his forehead.

"Don't look so surprised. Stan converted when he was thirty-two. He remained celibate the rest of his life. He had periods of intense longing and loneliness, I won't deny it. But I somehow felt like I had a front-row seat to watching him become more like Jesus. He had tasted Jesus, and nothing else mattered anymore."

"And you recommended he become a deacon?"

"I couldn't think of someone more qualified. Paul listed a number of sins when he wrote to the Corinthians, including that one. Then he said, 'And such were some of you.' A Christian is not defined by the sins of the past or the struggles of the present but by the vision of the future."

Chris was stunned.

Gil put his glasses back on and took a deep breath. "As easy as it would be to go along with the world on this one, I just can't. I know there are people who think I'm telling them not to be true to themselves. And they're right. The Christian preacher tells people all day long, 'Don't be true to yourself. The self you'd be true to is rotten to the core.' Authenticity isn't accepting your sins. It's admitting your sins and then being true to the person King Jesus has declared you to be."

"I feel better and worse at the same time," Chris said over the clanking of silverware in the soapy water of the sink. "Thanks."

Gil chuckled. "We're in a constant struggle. It feels good to fight sin, but we long for the day we'll be—how does the hymn go?— 'saved, to sin no more.'" Gil began to hum the hymn's tune.

Chris had to admit to himself that he was moved by Gil's love for Stan, by Jesus's love for Stan.

Suddenly Gil broke off his humming to say, "You mentioned this morning about how you were saved as a child."

"That's right," Chris said.

"I know you've been having doubts lately, wondering whether you even want to be a Christian anymore. This thing with Chase has been really bothering you. And there are other things, some that I'm sure you haven't even mentioned to me."

Chris put in, "I know I don't need to have every last little thing figured out if I'm going to stick it out as a follower of Jesus. But God has seemed so distant lately. My heart has been so cold." He stood still at the sink, looking out the window at the backyard.

From the table, Gil said with a curious intensity in his voice, "But there's an ember in your heart that flames up whenever it's about Jesus, doesn't it?"

An ember that flames up about Jesus. Was that really true? Chris decided it was. Since coming to his grandfather's house, he already felt freedom about not having to fake his struggles any longer, and being around his grandpa's authentic love for Jesus certainly did stir something in him. Maybe the dark, cold night of his soul was coming to an end. He felt a surge of happiness within. For a moment he felt a little like he did when he was thirteen and caught up in a sense of God's presence and love for him.

THE SOUND OF CHRIS'S PHONE ringing worked its way down the stairs and into the kitchen. "I'd better see who that is," he told Gil and excused himself. Once upstairs, he went into his room and saw the phone vibrating and ringing on the nightstand. He didn't recognize the number. "Hello?" he said.

"Chris," came the voice on the other line.

Chris knew the voice.

Without thinking twice, he ended the call and put the phone down on the bedspread, as if he had just touched a hot stove. His heart was beating up into his throat, and his hands froze into fists. It had been months since he'd heard that voice. He'd deleted the name from his contacts list and blocked all the numbers he had on record for him.

The phone rang again. Chris backed away, deliberating whether or not he ought to answer it. He let it go to voice mail.

The third time it rang, he decided to answer the call as brainlessly as he had hung up the first time.

"What do you want, Dad?"

wanted to hear your voice today. I was hoping we could talk." The voice on the line was quivering.

"Sure, Dad!" Chris replied, oozing sarcasm. "How about we have an old-fashioned father-son chat? There is plenty for us to talk about. What would you like to start with?"

"Chris—"

"Oh, I know! We could start with how you've ruined Mom's life and permanently scarred mine. Is that a good place? Or how about the fact that you skipped out on your own mother's funeral? Want me to fill you in on the details? Want to hear how peaceful she looked? How your father wept like a baby, with his son nowhere to be found to comfort him?"

There was a silence on the other end of the phone that somehow sounded anguished.

"Oh, who am I kidding?" Chris said. "Like you care about that, anyway."

"I do care," his father said hesitantly.

Chris was shaking but trying to retain his resolve. "You know what? I don't have time for this. *I'm* helping Grandpa this weekend," he said, emphasizing "I'm" to make Chris Sr. feel guilty.

"I know. I talked to your mom."

"Did she give you my number? Did she tell you to call? Or were you just lonely on New Year's Eve? Did you need something to take your mind off your train wreck of a life?"

"Chris, I didn't want the new year to begin without apologizing to you."

"Funny you'd pick this year, Dad. Kind of convenient, don't you think?"

Silence.

"First time you apologize is the year I find out the truth about you. The last nine new years, you've been perfectly content to let me look like a fool. The only one who hadn't figured out who you are and what you did." Chris's teeth were gritted and his fists were clenched. "Here you are, acting like the prodigal son who came to his senses— you're just sorry you got caught."

"I'm not asking for a second chance—"

"It's too late for that, anyway," Chris interrupted.

"I miss you."

Chris buried the mouthpiece of the phone in his sleeve and turned his head away. The only way he could keep from crying was to channel his sadness into anger.

"Stay away from me," he said. "And don't call this number again."

With that, he hung up the phone. For a moment, the only sound he could hear upstairs was the grandfather clock in the hallway. Chris looked around the room, trying to make sense of what had just happened. Then, in a fit of agony, he threw the phone across the room, where it bounced loudly off the window and fell onto the window seat. He grabbed his jacket from the chair and stomped down the stairs.

GIL WAS NO LONGER IN THE KITCHEN. He stood in the doorway to the front room, a concerned look on his face.

"Something wrong?"

"It was Dad," Chris said.

Gil nodded as Chris blazed past him toward the front door. Gil hobbled into the front room and propped himself up next to the recliner. Chris put his shoes on and tied the laces with a fury.

"H-he said he wanted t-to apologize," Chris stammered. "I guess he was feeling sorry for himself, it being New Year's Eve and all." *New Year's resolution number one: Make up with your stupid son,* he thought to himself. *Pull the wool over his eyes for another nine years.*

"Where are you going?" Gil asked quietly.

"I have to get out of here," Chris said.

"What did you say to him?"

Chris didn't hear any of his grandfather's questions, and he lost all sense of how incoherent he must sound. "I can't believe how easy he thinks it must be. That I should be able to forgive and forget, to move on. It's the same thing Ashley did to me. Like this whole thing with Dad was just something to get past so we could get on with everything else. Who knows? Mom probably agrees with Dad. She might have even told him to call me."

"*I* told him to call you."

It took a moment for those words to sink into Chris's consciousness. When they did, he felt rage swelling up inside him. "You did what?"

"About a week ago," Gil said calmly.

Chris trembled, so angry that he was unable to focus his eyes on his granddad still standing before him. He turned toward the door and took a deep breath. All this time they'd talked about everything, but Gil hadn't had the decency to tell him this about his dad.

Gil continued. "He came by on Christmas Day. Surprise to me.

He said he wanted to apologize for not returning my calls. He said he was sorry he didn't show up for your grandma's funeral. It wasn't that he didn't want to go. He knew he would see all the people he had hurt all in one place, and he couldn't bear it. I think he's going through some kind of change of heart. He asked me to forgive him for all the trouble he'd caused."

Chris turned and faced his granddad. With disbelief in his voice, he muttered, "And I guess you forgave him?"

Gil didn't respond, but his eyes said it all. "I told him he ought to call you, your mom, and all the other people he'd hurt."

"You made him do this?" Chris was seething with resentment. He couldn't believe how quickly his grandfather had found it in his heart to make amends with the man who had ruined so many lives. The man deserved revenge, not restoration.

He looked at Gil standing there stooped over, supporting himself with his cane, and felt nothing but animosity. He heard himself piece together words he never thought he'd say: "You are a pathetic old man. A weak…miserable…coward."

With that, Chris flung open the door, fled from the house, and ran to his car. He backed out of the driveway so fast he almost hit the mailbox. And then he took off down the street, showing no concern about the remaining ice on the road.

FROM THE FRONT DOOR, Gil watched his grandson's car turn the corner and speed off into the distance as the sun was sinking below the horizon. With tears in his eyes, he turned back toward his empty living room, fumbling with the switch that would have turned the porch light on. Then he shook his head, remembering it was out and hadn't been replaced. He couldn't even leave the light on for his grandson to return.

He was hurt by Chris's remarks, but he chose to consider the counsel he'd often given in situations like these. *Hurt people hurt people.* Besides, he'd said things out of anger before himself.

What was more concerning to Gil was not the harsh words but the path his grandson might take. Before this weekend began, Gil had hoped his time with Chris would be a positive influence on his grandson. He hoped he could offer some wisdom and direction as Chris faced important choices for his future. But now those hopes seemed shattered. He worried that he had done more harm than good.

Gil shuffled toward his desk in the corner. He sat down in the chair, put his head in his hands, and began to weep. He was not mourning his wife, his illness, or his loneliness. This time he was bearing the sorrow of his grandson. In those quiet moments, when the stillness of the house set in and the winter evening sent a chill through everything, Gil cried out to God, asking for strength and wisdom. From his heart poured his own regrets, his failures as a father, his decisions that had caused unintended pain. And then he interceded for his grandson.

THE MOST FRUSTRATING PART about driving through Lewisville was that there was so little to drive through. More than once the car had swerved due to the ice on the road or the tears blinding Chris's eyes.

He felt guilty. How had he lashed out so terribly, when his grandfather was the last person he'd want to hurt? But then he remembered his father, the pain he'd caused, and chose to focus not on the ways he was a perpetrator but rather the ways he was a victim.

He headed out of town to the open, winding country roads. They were snowy and slushy, but they had the advantage of being as lonely as Chris felt. For more than an hour, he drove. Aimlessly. He kept rehearsing his conversations with his father and grandfather, a process that heated up his anger...until his sense of mistreatment started getting worn out like gum that had been chewed so much it lost its flavor.

Gradually he began to cool down. And to realize he was hungry. And more than hungry, he was thirsty. He headed the car back into town to find a place to get a drink. Remembering that it was New Year's Eve, he worried he might run into a drunk driver. Then again, he thought he might be one before night's end. ·

Downtown, there was only one place where anything was happening, a sports bar named Mike's Bar & Grill. Chris parked the car and made his way inside. The lighting was dim, but the music was loud. He took a seat at the bar and waited to be served.

"What'll it be?" said the bartender, a bald-headed man who was wiping down the area behind the cash register.

"I'll need a few minutes," Chris said. He couldn't think straight. Part of him wanted to get smashing drunk, while another part of him wanted to find a hole to climb in and die. His head was pounding.

In the corner of the bar was a television with live coverage of Times Square as partygoers awaited the countdown to New Year's. Dozens of happy faces graced the TV screen. People eagerly awaiting a new year, a new start, a new life. The party atmosphere in the restaurant wasn't much different. There were a few who'd already had too much to drink, but most everyone was there in groups of two or three or four. New Year's Eve. Memories in the making. Meanwhile, Chris had never felt so alone.

The previous year had brought its share of challenges. Last New Year's Eve, he and Ashley had been on top of Lookout Mountain with some college friends. They'd hiked all day and spent the evening watching the stars and talking about their plans. Since then, Chris had proposed *and* broken off their engagement. So much for plans.

In one year's time, Chris had finished school and was considering more classes. He'd gone to visit his grandparents one month, only to bury Grandma Frances the next. He'd been all in with the core team of a church start-up, only to discover the core of his faith crumbling. And then there was his father and the embarrassment of discovering the awful truth everyone else already knew. The rage threatened to come back.

Chris suddenly decided what he wanted to drink. "Long Island iced tea," Chris said to the bartender. Lots of liquor and still tasted good. He was going to have a solo New Year's party for the ages.

Chris felt his fingers tighten around the restaurant menu. No, he would not open his heart again. He never wanted to be let down that way again, to feel the pain of lost love. Love only complicated life. It caused him to hurt Ashley, his mother, and now his grandpa—a man who had always loved Chris unconditionally. He knew what he had to do. He would march back to his granddad's house, gather his things, say good-bye, and leave well enough alone. He would not apologize. To forgive was to play the fool. He would not seek any more help. He would not believe. He would start a new life without Ashley or anybody else who would stand in his way. Faith was too big of a risk, and love too much of a struggle.

It felt a fierce kind of good to have that settled.

THE CHILL OF THE NIGHT AIR rushed through the restaurant and swept by Chris's face. Annoyed that someone must be keeping the door open, Chris turned to see who was coming into the bar. Standing at the entrance, barely visible through the haze of smoke and dimness of light, was an old man with a scarf hung loosely around his neck. He was leaning on a wooden cane. Chris squinted in disbelief. It was Gil, scanning the restaurant, looking for a sign of his grandson.

The thoughts that flew through Chris's mind in that moment were so many it would take hours to process them all. First, the questions. *What is he doing here? Who drove him? What kind of effort did it take for him to venture out alone? Is he crazy? What if he were to fall again?*

And then, as the answers fell into place, one on top of another, Chris began shaking his head. He pushed away from the bar and stepped down onto the floor. Moving past the tables of raucous partygoers, he made his way toward his granddad until the two of them caught each other's eyes.

Gil nodded in the direction of the bar. Then he hobbled over on his cane and attempted to climb up onto the barstool. Chris helped him up.

"What are you doing here?"

"Just out celebrating New Year's," he said with a smile. "Didn't expect to see you here."

"Sure. How did you get here?" Chris felt terrible, causing his elderly grandpa to come traipsing out into the cold after him.

"I have my ways."

"Well, you shouldn't have come," Chris said. "I'm fine."

"I didn't say you weren't fine."

"You should be at home."

"There's not a party going on at home. Watching the ball drop by yourself just isn't the same, you know?" He winked.

Chris sat back and took in the irony of sitting at a bar with Gil, the teetotaling pastor, the sage of Lewisville.

The bartender approached again. "Long Island for you as well?" he asked Gil.

"I'll take a regular sweet tea," Gil answered. "Oh, and some hot wings for us. I've been craving those for a while."

Chris shook his head and wanted to crawl under a rock.

"You came to preach to me, is that it?" Chris said. "Come on, let me have it."

"Nope," Gil said. "There is a time for preaching, but this is not it." He took his straw out of the wrapper and stuck it in his sweet tea.

"Well, what is this the time for, then?"

"Tea and hot wings, I believe."

"So you're gonna sit here and watch me get plastered?"

"I'm gonna sit here with you no matter what you do."

Chris didn't say anything for a few minutes, and they distracted themselves with the TV. Then the hot wings came, another welcome distraction. All the while, Chris felt as though his earlier stubbornness, his resolve to never ask forgiveness and never seek restoration, looked silly when placed next to the warmth and wisdom of his grandfather. He was embarrassed by his tantrum and wanted to put it out of his mind.

Finally Chris turned to Gil. "I'm really sorry for what I said."

"It's already forgotten."

"No, really, I am so sorry," he continued, stirring his drink. "I don't know what I was thinking. My anger got the best of me."

"Do you know what 'forgotten' means?" Gil said. "It means you can stop apologizing."

"I owe you an explanation at least."

"You don't owe me anything."

"So you just dismiss what I said to you? Just sweep it under the rug like it didn't happen?"

"Oh no. I didn't say that," Gil answered.

"I'm confused, then."

"What you said hurt me, of course. Even knowing that it was your anger speaking. Minimizing and dismissing doesn't accomplish anything."

"So, how do you forgive so quickly?"

"It's not easy. We are not as forgetful as God, unfortunately."

Chris turned toward Gil with a confused look.

"You know, Jeremiah 31. 'For I will forgive their iniquity, and I will remember their sin no more.' Isn't that a glorious promise? That God won't ever bring up our sin again? Takes a lifetime of determination to get that truth planted deep in your heart. We commit to memory. God commits to forgetfulness."

"So you forgive me?"

"I've been forgiven for far more than what you did against me by saying a few hurtful words. I can't withhold grace from you."

Chris picked up his drink and took a big gulp. "Well, thank you. I really regret what I said to you."

Gil picked up a hot wing, took a few bites, then sat it back down.

"I really regret not having been a better father to your dad."

Chris was taken aback. "What do you mean?"

"Just what I said."

"No way," Chris said. "No way I'm accepting that Dad turned out the way he did because you were a bad father. You can be proud of Aunt Ruth. Even if Dad—"

"I can't take credit for Ruth," Gil said. "She's a jewel because of Frances. And because God is gracious."

"I don't think she'd say that. She'd give you credit too."

"It's only by grace that any kid ever turns out all right."

"Maybe so. But you can't say you weren't a good dad and leave it at that."

"Well, then," Gil said. "Since you are going to parse my regrets—"

"I just don't get it," Chris said. "How could Dad grow up in the house with you and Grandma and come to abandon everything you believe in?"

"I don't know that he's abandoned everything," Gil said.

"Well, he abandoned Mom."

The two stayed quiet for a couple of minutes.

"Well, I still regret some things I did and some things I didn't do. Early on, I had my priorities all mixed up. I would often let ministry become my idol and neglect my family much more than I should. I cheated them in that regard. Failed to see them as my primary ministry."

"That's nothing compared to Dad," Chris said. "He doesn't deserve to be mentioned in the same sentence as you."

"Sin is sin, Chris," Gil said. "We're all in the same sentence. And my regrets are my regrets. But thank you for your kindness." He picked up his half-eaten hot wing.

Chris finished his drink and slurped the bottom, then set it down on the counter.

"Another?" the bartender asked. Chris thought for a second and glanced at Gil. "I'll just take a water, please."

"Sure thing."

"And another plate of wings," Gil said to the man. "Still hungry." He rubbed his stomach.

"Shouldn't we get you home?"

"After we eat a bit more."

It took Chris a minute, but then he realized what was going on. Gil thought he'd be too intoxicated to drive after one drink. He struggled not to laugh.

"Okay, sounds good. I didn't know you had such an appetite."

"You know me," Gil said. "I'm a growing boy."

AS THEY WAITED ON the fresh wings, Chris chimed in with another thing he'd been thinking about. "You know what's funny? In all my doubts and questions, I don't have a problem at all with hell—the very thing that most people I know have the biggest issue with."

"That's not surprising," Gil said.

"It's not?"

"Surprising? No. Interesting? Yes."

"I'm confused."

"I remember an African missionary visiting our church, I don't know, maybe fifteen years ago. We hosted him in our home. The room you're staying in. Anyway, he was telling me about what was controversial in the tribe he was working in. Very different from here."

"Hell wasn't a problem for them?"

"Not at all. The idea of God as a judge? They had that down pat."

"So what was their big hang-up?"

"The idea of loving your enemies and turning the other cheek. It didn't fit with their sense of justice, of retribution. They had the hardest time swallowing that."

"Huh," Chris said. "No one has a problem with turning the other cheek around here."

"I wouldn't say no one," Gil said gently. "Because you do." He looked up at Chris, but he said nothing.

Chris just sat there.

"There are many cultures in the world that have no problem with the idea of wrath and punishment," Gil said. "In their minds it is completely understandable. Right now you line up with them because you're all in favor of wrath being poured out on your father."

The bartender picked the perfect time to drop off the wings, giving Chris a breather.

"Does that hit close to home?"

"Nah, you're way off," Chris said, red faced and smiling. "I don't know where you come up with this crazy stuff."

Gil laughed, then picked up another wing to munch on. "If your dad gets to heaven, it will be the same way you do. Through King Jesus. And totally undeserved."

"By the way, I thought you said you weren't going to preach tonight." Chris gently slapped him on the arm.

"I'm not preaching. I'm talking. And you're the one that got me started."

"I assume the next sermon is going to be about how I have to forgive Dad. That I've been forgiven for more than I'll ever have to forgive. That grace comes first, right?"

"It sounds like you're preaching to yourself, so there's no need," Gil said, winking. "You're a quick learner."

In a short while, Gil said, "Well, I'm full and tired. Can't party as long as I used to. Ready to drive us home?"

Gil paid the bill, and they ventured out into the cold.

AS THEY LEFT DOWNTOWN, the condition of the roads worsened. The slush on the side of the road was beginning to refreeze now that the sun was down, and when Chris drove close to the edge, they could hear the crunching sound, as if they were driving on rocks.

Chris happened to glance at the digital clock on the car radio. 8:52. That sparked a memory. Something he'd read in the local newspaper earlier that day.

He glanced over at Gil. "You're not really all that tired are you, Gramps? You can stay up a few more minutes, right?" he asked.

"I guess so," said Gil. "Why?"

"You'll see."

A minute later Chris took a turn onto a side road. The ice on this road was, if anything, worse than on the other. But in less than a mile, Chris had navigated them to the top of a bare hill where he had liked to go when on visits to his grandparents as a boy. He stopped the car and killed the ignition.

"Now, what's going on? What are we doing here?" Gil inquired.

"I'll help you get out," Chris said.

Moments later, they were both leaning against the side of the car, overlooking the lights of the town. Gil took a deep breath and looked up at the more impressive display of starlight in the sky. "Another beautiful clear night."

He didn't seem to notice there were more cars and motion near the lake at the town's largest park, three miles away, than one would expect on a winter evening. But Chris did.

Then suddenly a pink firework like a sky carnation opened up over the lake.

"Oh!" said Gil in surprise.

"Oh yes," said Chris.

More fireworks appeared in the sky, some bloomers like the first one, some whizzers, and some flashing boomers. They were far enough away to barely hear the crackle of the fireworks, but close enough to see the brilliant lights.

Gil sighed. "I love fireworks."

"I happened to read about this in the paper," Chris explained. "This is your Fourth of July display, actually. Because of the drought last summer, the officials wouldn't allow fireworks. So the city postponed the celebration until New Year's Eve."

"Good for us," said Gil.

They sat in silence for a few minutes and enjoyed the sparkling sky.

Finally Gil broke the silence. "Chris, I want you to know that I'm proud of you."

Chris felt a tightness in his chest. "Proud? Of what? Me running off to drink away my problems? Breaking off an engagement to a perfect girl? Backing out of a church plant?"

"Stop," Gil said, interrupting. "I'm proud of the young man you are becoming. You've come face to face with some devastating sin and hypocrisy. You're asking big questions and wrestling with important things, and there's no shame in that. You want to own your own faith, not satisfied to go through the motions of a faith you've inherited. That's admirable, if you ask me."

"Well, I appreciate that, Gramps. But I don't feel very admirable."

A grand finale of shooting fireworks, and the display was over. Chris helped the older man into the car and started for home.

"Thanks for a fun New Year's party tonight," Gil said as they passed through the doorway into his home. "But I really must go to bed now. Tomorrow I want us to visit the cemetery."

Monday, January 1

Chris slept soundly all night. When he opened the shades in the morning, the sunlight streamed into his room. The clear blue sky against the backdrop of the remaining snow made the hill outside look like something from a children's fairy tale.

Feeling rested, he went downstairs and decided to cut up some fruit and put together a fruit salad. He would make some extra so that his grandfather could have the leftovers later. He planned on leaving later that day, needing to get back to work after the holiday. Aunt Ruth had agreed to come and be with Gil on New Year's night.

He spent some time sitting at the kitchen table, drinking coffee and soaking in the quiet grace of the old house, not hearing a peep from Gil. He felt a dull regret for running off the day before and giving his grandpa so much distress. Hopefully Gil would be able to sleep well into the day. And maybe the surprise Chris had arranged after getting home last night would help to make up for what he had said and done.

He thought about how lucky he was to have a man like Gil in his life. And then he grew sad thinking about the fact that he wouldn't have him for much longer. Gil was getting to that age when it becomes increasingly likely there won't be another New Year's.

Suddenly he heard the old man rustling around, then the television coming on in Gil's room. *Funny how I haven't missed technology,* he thought. A weekend unplugged, and yet he felt more energized than he had when he arrived.

A few minutes later, Gil appeared at the threshold of the kitchen. "Happy New Year!" he said cheerfully. He walked over to the table and sat down. "The weatherman says the warmup is finally coming."

"Breakfast is served!" Chris said, divvying out generous portions of fruit salad onto their plates.

"Ah!" Gil said, eyeing the fruit. Using his spoon, he played around with the fruit, turning them over and separating them. "It's wonderful to think that God could have made our food bland but, no, He gives us all kinds of food that taste wonderful and look beautiful."

They took a few bites before Chris said, "Hey, I was thinking about something you said yesterday. About all your life's work being stored in that big box upstairs."

"Don't take me too seriously," Gil said. "The real work pastors like me do isn't putting words on a page. It's putting the Word in people's hearts. The people who listened to those sermons—they're my real life's work."

"Sure." Chris nodded and then cut to the chase. "Does it bother you that your ministry is over?"

"My ministry isn't over until I die," Gil said.

"You know what I mean—your work in the church. How are you coping now that you've been put on the shelf? It takes so much energy just for you to get out of bed and sit in a chair to read. All those sermon outlines in that box. Doesn't it bother you that you worked all your life for the Lord and now you're past your sell-by date?"

"You're not much for sugarcoating things, are you?" Gil said, shoving his elbow in Chris's direction playfully.

"I was just wondering. What it must feel like to have given everything to Jesus for years and then be done, just stuck at home doing finger exercises."

Gil was quiet for a moment. Then he quoted from Jesus. "Rejoice not, that the spirits are subject unto you; but rather rejoice, because your names are written in heaven." He tapped his cane on the floor in front of his seat. "I will be content. He is my reward. Not ministry or success or productivity."

Chris could tell from the way Gil said it that it was as much a resolution as it was a declaration. "Preaching to yourself there?"

"Every day," Gil said. "I've fought my entire life to find my worth and value in what Christ has done for me, not in what I do for Christ. There were times, I'm sorry to say, I mostly lost that fight."

Aside from some small talk, they ate the rest of their breakfast in a blessed silence. As Chris got up to wash the dishes, he turned to say over his shoulder, "You still want to visit Grandma's grave?"

GIL WAS HAVING SECOND THOUGHTS. The ease with which he'd tumbled to the floor the day before, along with his evening adventure, made him wonder if it were such a good idea to go the cemetery. The ice was melting, and Chris had cleared the sidewalk and driveway. But things were still slick. One wrong move, one chip of ice, or one misplaced rock could cause him to fall. And hitting the ground would be much worse than falling onto the carpet in his room. Chris, though, seemed oblivious to the dangers. *Must be nice,* Gil thought, *to never worry about hurting yourself.*

Chris helped Gil put on his overcoat. Gil had on two pairs of pants; first because he didn't want to be cold, and second because it would provide extra cushion in case he fell.

For a second he wondered if he ought to take the fancy walker in the kitchen instead of the cane. Which was more important? Being dignified or being safer?

Chris brought him the cane. Decision made.

"Thank you much," Gil said. They walked together to the door and out onto the front porch. The air was warmer than he expected. There was still a lot of snow and ice, but it was turning to slush all around them. The driveway and sidewalk were completely dry, however, thanks to the efforts of his grandson two nights before.

Chris opened the passenger side door for Gil and beckoned him toward his seat. It wasn't difficult to get in, thankfully, and Gil propped up his cane between his legs. Once Chris got in, he said, "You'll have to remind me just where the cemetery is."

"Just a couple of miles away, on the edge of town. I'll direct you."

The roads were mostly clear, but everything else was still white. There was almost no activity in town, as if the entire town were sleeping in.

"Here it is—on the right," Gil said as they approached Welch Memorial Cemetery, with its two large pillars on either side of the road. The snow-covered ground made Gil feel at peace. He never liked coming to see Frances's grave and noticing how fresh the dirt was. Today he wouldn't have to. God had blanketed her grave with snow.

Chris drove up the hill and around the main circle. Finally, Gil put his hand up. "This is it," he said. A pang of loneliness swept his heart whenever he came to her grave. This was the first day of the first full year they would not be together.

Chris put the car in park and turned off the engine. Silence. A couple of birds could be heard in the distance, but other than that, the only sound was the wind blowing. Chris came around to Gil's side of the car and opened the door. Frances's grave was right next to the road.

"You don't have to get out if you don't want to, Gramps."

"I know," Gil said. "That's why I had you come around the circle the long way, so we'd wind up with the passenger side next to her grave." He continued to sit in the passenger seat with the door open.

The stone was for both of them, but only Frances's death date was chiseled in. "September 9," Gil said. "To think, all those years, September 9 was just like any other day. Never knew that on that date I'd lose her." He could feel his chest tightening. Chris was standing quietly at the foot of the grave.

Memories flooded Gil's mind. Memories of the day they'd put his dear Frances in the ground. They had stood around her grave, recalling her life. Celebrating her legacy. The pastor had said a few words—just the right mixture of pathos and humor. Everyone else had left before the burial was finished. But Gil had stayed behind, wanting to make sure everything was done just right. He had soaked an old handkerchief with his tears. He had wanted to make sure the coffin holding his wife's lifeless body was carefully planted in the soil, awaiting the promised spring. When the death of winter would give way to new life.

Interrupting Gil's thoughts, Chris came alongside him and squeezed his arm. They remained together in one of those silences too holy for words for a while. Gil broke the silence when, out of gritted teeth and with a sort of seething anger welling up inside of him, he said quietly but firmly, "I hate death."

Chris didn't say anything. He seemed taken aback by Gil's display of emotion, to the point that Gil felt he needed to justify himself.

"I've done so many funerals." He leaned forward on his cane and looked out over the graveyard. "I know so many people buried on these grounds. I've stood in this place with wives burying their husbands, the women standing in the very spot where I'd bury them too, years later."

Chris let out a deep sigh.

Gil wondered if his grandson, at twenty-two, had any sense of how quickly life is over. Of how important it is to live for King Jesus and not for what doesn't matter, before it's too late. He hoped Chris would put all his troubles in eternal perspective, placing his questions and doubts on the scales of eternity in order to see how one's vision for the future affects one's actions in the present.

Gil continued, "I hate how death snatches away young people in their prime. Or how it waits patiently, until the years chip away at our strength. I've seen how time batters and bends the backs of even the heartiest soldiers, until death sneaks in and takes them away. Some of the toughest men I've ever known are buried here."

Chris walked over to the gravestone and wiped the snow and slush off the top. "I miss her too," he said.

"Death doesn't wait until love runs out," Gil said. He felt a fire in his heart as he spoke. "It's an intruder in our homes. We worked hard to build a home of joy and peace. And death shattered it." Gil thought of how Frances grew ill. How fast it all happened.

"What does Paul say? 'The last enemy to be destroyed is death,' I think," Chris said.

"Yes—that is exactly what he said. Indeed," Gil responded. His clenched fist loosened a little.

"Frances loved Easter so much. She loved singing about it. There was one particular sunrise service we did years ago... I still remember how her eyes looked. It was as though she saw something I couldn't fully grasp. As if she were privileged to be in on some fine secret. But the secret was the one we all know. She was just especially caught up by it that day, I guess. Moments like that I'll never forget. Fifty-six years of grace. I miss my angel."

The songbirds had flown away, and only the wind could be heard.

AS GIL SAT IN THE CAR, facing Frances's gravestone, he remembered sitting next to her in the hospital, reading the Scriptures to her. For days she was unable to speak. The stroke was much more severe than Gil's had been. The only way she was able to communicate was by moving her eyes or moaning softly. Whenever Gil opened up the Scriptures and began to read, she convulsed in tears. Her mouth contorted into the best smile she could muster. Even as she was in the throes of death, the stroke could not hold back the smile behind the mask. Behind that stroke-frozen face, hope was winning. Gil could see it. It was the expression of a woman who, even while singing the somber, sad verse of death, couldn't hide her anticipation of the resurrection refrain that was coming. Love that is stronger than death.

The last passage he read to her was from Romans 8: "In all these things we are more than conquerors through him that loved us. For I am persuaded, that neither death, nor life, nor angels, nor principalities, nor powers, nor things present, nor things to come, nor height, nor depth, nor any other creature, shall be able to separate us from the love of God, which is in Christ Jesus our Lord."

The nurses said it would probably be her last night. Journey's end. No one ever thinks about the gravity of saying "till death do us part" until death is on the doorstep, waiting to part the best of friends. For an hour after she died, Gil held her hand, wanting to hold on until the last of her warmth faded away.

The pastor's message at the graveside was about tears and laughter and how the death of a saint brings both. Tears for our loss. Laughter for heaven's gain. Tears for our present pain. Laughter for our future hope.

"Today is hard," Gil broke the silence. "But today doesn't have the last word."

Chris walked back to the car and stood next to Gil.

"Enough with sadness," Gil said. "You know something?"

"What's that?"

"It doesn't matter how tightly they closed her coffin. They encased it in bronze, locked it up tight, and dumped six feet of dirt on top of it. But it doesn't matter. That casket will be no match for the power of the resurrection on the Last Day." Gil put one arm outside the car and his other arm on top of the car door so he could hoist himself into a standing position, as if to defy his weakness. "Those locks will be undone. The decomposition of her old body will be reversed."

Chris took his grandpa's arm in his.

"You know something else? The soil we're watering today with our tears—this is the garden where her resurrection body will spring to life." Gil felt a conviction deep within him that gave him an unusual confidence on his feet. "It may be winter, but spring is coming."

With that, Gil forced his feet forward into the slushy grass, steadying himself with his cane. He kissed the palm of his hand, then planted that kiss directly on top of her gravestone. He felt a lone tear trickle down his cheek, leaving a tiny pathway that caught the coldness of the winter wind. He tasted a hint of saltiness as it made its way down to his lips. He was smiling.

"Tears and laughter today," he said. "Only laughter tomorrow."

As Chris pulled into Gil's driveway after returning from the cemetery, Gil spotted several cars parked at the curb in front of his house. "That's Ron's car," he said. "And I think I recognize a couple of those others. What's going on?"

Chris smiled. "Let's go in and see."

Moments later, through the glass in the front door, they could make out the familiar face of Ron Thurmond. "Happy New Year!" Ron shouted from inside, tapping on the window.

"I knew we should've locked the door," Gil said, smiling. "Did you know about this?"

"Know about it?" Chris said. "I planned it!" He laughed to himself, remembering the business card Ron had given him with his number on it. He was supposed to call him if Gil needed anything. It turned out that he did need something—an old-fashioned jam session for his grandpa on New Year's morning, just like they used to have when Chris was young. Chris knew how much his grandfather had enjoyed those times. But there hadn't been anything like a party in the house since Frances had died.

Once Chris had helped Gil up the steps and through the door, they saw the front room filled with Ron and twenty or so mostly older men and women. A few of the adults had brought children with them. "Well, I do declare!" said Gil loudly. There was a twinkle in his eye.

Gil introduced Chris around. These were all people Gil had known for years, fellow church members, friends, and neighbors. All rounded up by Ron to join in the party. Chris was thrilled by how many had showed up on short notice on a holiday—another testimony to his grandfather's popularity.

"Nice to see you again," said Ron to Chris. "Don't be expecting any 'balance' when the music gets started!" Ron laughed.

"This is definitely a time for passion instead, isn't it?" Chris laughed too.

Gil introduced Chris to two older men and a young woman he knew from Mount Zion Baptist. The young woman's name was Sheree, and she gave off as hip a vibe as anybody Chris knew in the city. When he learned that Sheree was the music director at Mount Zion, known for its high-intensity services, he anticipated even more the music that was about to come.

"And this is Katherine Reed," said Gil as a handsome dark-haired woman in middle age came up to them.

Katy! said Chris to himself. "Hi, Katherine. We talked on the phone." He could easily recognize her face from the church-directory pictures he'd seen, despite the passage of years. He wondered if, during her troubled teen years, her parents would have ever believed that she could turn into a beaming, confident, professional woman.

"I'm so glad you've come to stay with your grandpa," she said to Chris. "He's rather special to all of us."

"Not more special than he is to me," said Chris.

Just as the mood threatened to get too serious, Katherine took Gil's arm and pretended to tug him away. "Come on, Gil, let's go do those therapies!"

"Oh no! I thought I was getting a day off!" said Gil, playing along.

Right then Ron cued the musicians and the room erupted in sound. First up was a guitar ensemble ripping off an up-tempo version of "I've Got a Tiger by the Tail." Then came a rendition of "He Stopped Loving Her Today" that brought tears to a couple of old faces. Next, one of the men sang "The Richest Man (in the World)," accompanied by fiddle and guitar. This was followed by some amateurish stop-and-start performances and some trying out of banjos and mandolins. Finally, Sheree stepped in to teach the group some of the new gospel hits and got the whole group swaying and clapping to the music.

In the midst of it all, Chris kept an eye on the kids running in and out of the room. *I was just like that not so long ago,* he thought. His mind could well remember it. His heart now could too.

A jam session in this house never took place without food. And so, spread out on the table in the dining room were plates of roasted chicken, homemade casseroles, several small containers with various vegetables, cornbread, and several kinds of pie and cake. Whenever anyone wanted something, they just loaded up one of Grandma Frances's china plates and brought it back into the front room to listen to the music while they ate.

Chris was just coming back from the dining room with a second plateful when he heard Gil say to the musicians, "Can I make a request?"

"Absolutely," one of the women replied. "If we don't know the song, we'll just wing it!"

"Then let's have 'Come, Lord'!" Gil said.

"I know the one you're talking about," Ronald said. "Wasn't that Frances's favorite?" He sat at her piano, opened up her hymnal, and began to play. Most of the others closed around the piano and joined with Ron in singing. Chris just listened. To him, it was almost as if his grandmother were with them. Tears formed in Gil's eyes as the voices filled the room.

> Come, for creation groans,
> Impatient of Thy stay,
> Worn out with these long years of ill,
> These ages of delay.
>
> Come, for love waxes cold;
> Its steps are faint and slow:
> Faith now is lost in unbelief,
> Hope's lamp burns dim and low.
>
> Come, and make all things new;
> Build up this ruined earth,
> Restore our faded Paradise,
> Creation's second birth.

After a good three hours of eating, singing, and joke telling, the boisterous occasion came to an end. As they left the house, the guests laughed and waved, calling out "Happy New Year!" and "We love you, Pastor Gil!" They sang all the way down the sidewalk and even after they were in their cars.

Gil stayed seated for a few minutes, silent, head bowed, seeming to bask in the afterglow of their joyful presence. Chris, meanwhile, slipped away to pack.

IT WAS MIDAFTERNOON, and Chris had the drive back to Knoxville ahead of him. Upstairs, he stuffed his few belongings into his duffel bag, made the bed in his room, and took one last look out the picture window at the glistening scene of melting snow. Then he walked across the hall to shut the door to the closet he had left open in his aunt Ruth's room two nights before. He wanted to leave everything just the way he'd found it. It was the least he could do.

As he headed toward the stairs, he passed the doorway to his father's room. Immediately he stopped still and dropped his gaze to the floor. He hadn't been able to so much as look into this room since he'd come on this visit to his grandfather's, and he wasn't sure he would be able to now. He took some deep breaths. Finally he dropped his duffel bag to the floor, turned, and walked in.

The room was very nearly as his father had left it when he had moved out in the 1970s—which was just the way Chris had always liked it on previous visits. Chris walked past the bed with its childish coverlet and looked at the pictures of his father and his father's friends on the wall, then ran his finger along a shelf with a baseball glove, a tennis racket with badly sprung strings, and a stack of yellowing superhero comic books. He bent his knees before a low bookcase and read the spines of adventure novels and mysteries, along with what Chris had never thought much about before—a Bible, devotional books, and other Christian reading. His father had been a devout youth, it seemed, whatever he had turned into later.

Chris felt the anger that had seized him ever since he had learned of his father's betrayal begin to lose its grip. He didn't know if he could ever forgive his father or love him again as he once had. He didn't know what he would do if his father called again. But the room reminded him that his father was a normal human being. Not a saint. Not a devil. Instead, someone who once seemed to have aspirations to follow Jesus, just as he had. Someone whose failings were all too obvious, just as his were.

Slipping into hypocrisy, as his father had done, would be easy, however strenuously he might resist. Giving up on faith altogether, or turning religion into an impersonal intellectual exercise, would be easy enough too. Really living his faith, as Gil had for six decades, would be a lot tougher. War, as Gil had called it. But after spending three days in this house, now it seemed like a war that might be worth fighting.

Chris still had lots of unanswered questions, but he felt there might actually be answers to those questions, even if he hadn't discovered them all yet. He didn't see eye to eye with his granddad on everything, and probably never would. Even so, he wanted to be like Gil when he got to that age. Firm in his convictions, sophisticated in his arguments, yet without the rigidity that comes from a hardened heart.

Ashley had been right. Coming here to Lewisville and talking to his grandfather about his doubts had been just what he needed.

Ashley. What was he going to do about her? Did he love her? He knew better now than ever that he did. And he knew that she loved him too. But she would never marry him if he were to walk away from his faith. Nor would he want her to.

On one side were Jesus and Ashley.

On the other, an obscure vision of himself. Alone.

Inside his father's room, the stillness made him feel like he had muffs over his ears. Tree branches waved noiselessly outside the window as if on a TV screen with the volume turned off. Dust motes hung in the air where they were caught by sunlight entering through the window. Chris stayed there thinking for a long time.

FINALLY CHRIS CAME DOWN the staircase with his duffel bag in his hand.

"Now, what's your hurry?" Gil said. He was standing in the hallway by the front room.

"I'm not in a hurry, Gramps," Chris said.

"You don't have to be at work at that trucking place until tomorrow, right? So why not stay until after dinner?"

"I'd like to. But…well…there's this girl I need to talk to."

Gil smiled. "Then, by all means, you need to be on your way."

Chris bit his lip and hoped he would have many more visits with his granddad.

Gil said, "You'll keep in touch, right? I want to hear how things go. With everything."

"I will, I will. That is, if I can find a way to beat Mom to the punch." Gil laughed at that.

Chris walked past him into the front room. He noticed the recliner still sitting there right near the door where he'd put it earlier during the jam session. "Oh, I'll help you move that back," he said. He put down his duffel bag and was about to drag the recliner back to its normal place, when he felt a hand on his shoulder.

"Wait."

Chris looked up into the wrinkled face of his granddad.

"Kneel down," Gil said. No hint of a request. This was a command. He motioned for Chris to move around to the front of the chair.

Chris wasn't sure what Gil was doing. Kneel down? He walked around the chair and got down on his knees. His elbows sunk into the soft cushion of the seat. Meanwhile, his grandfather put down his cane and shuffled over to the side of the recliner. He steadied himself with one hand on the chair and the other hand on Chris's shoulders.

"I want to bless you, Chris."

Chris felt his body start to quiver. His hand began to tremble, and for a moment he considered protesting. He didn't think of himself as deserving of such a thing. But then he sensed tears welling up in his eyes. The awkwardness of the moment was overcome by his craving for affirmation and guidance.

He bowed his head and felt the warmth of his grandfather's hand on his back, pressing into him gently, firmly. It seemed as if he were holding up his grandfather, but in another way, it was as if his grandfather were holding up him.

"May King Jesus bless you and keep you, Christopher Walker," Gil said. His voice was strong.

"May King Jesus make His face shine upon you and be gracious to you.

"May the Lord turn His face toward you and give you peace.

"Our Father in heaven, everlasting Father of the fatherless, heaven is Your throne and the earth is Your footstool. The heavens declare Your glory, and the sky above proclaims Your handiwork.

"Be Chris's Shepherd and carry him forever. Help Chris to know Your ways, O Lord. Teach him Your paths. Teach him to do Your will. Let Your good Spirit lead him on level ground.

"Give him each day his daily bread. We know You, O God, to be the One who will supply his every need according to Your riches in glory in Christ Jesus.

"Restore us both; let Your face shine, that we may be saved. For the glory of Your name, deliver us and atone for our sins, for Your name's sake. You are our steadfast love and our fortress, our stronghold and our deliverer.

"In the powerful and glorious name of King Jesus, amen."

Chris gently moved up to a standing position. He looked at his granddad and saw him smile back at him.

And then Gil said it. "I love you, Chris." What he always made sure to tell Chris.

"Love you too, Gramps. Thank you."

Chris handed him his cane. Then he pushed the recliner back into place, picked up his duffel bag, and headed to the door.

"Thanks again for coming," Gil said. "I needed you around this weekend."

I need you more than you need me, Chris thought. "I'll be back soon."

And with that he decided not to linger any longer. He walked down the front porch, got in the car, threw the duffel bag into the backseat, and pulled out of the driveway. He could see the silhouette of his granddad from behind the screen door, waving to him from inside the house.

The sky was clear and the sun was out.

Conversation Guide

1. *Clear Winter Nights* is the story of a young man who has begun questioning the Christian faith he previously took for granted. Describe your spiritual journey so far.

2. Have you ever been through a "dark night of the soul" when you felt separated from God? If so, what was it like?

3. When it comes to faith in God, what are you having doubts or questions about?

4. Chris's fiancée, Ashley, encourages him to talk about his spiritual doubts with a trusted older adult. Who do you feel you can open up to safely about the deepest issues you're struggling with?

5. The recent revelation of his father's betrayal of his mother has been the biggest blow to Chris's faith. How has the hypocrisy of Christians made it harder for you to believe in Jesus?

6. Where do you stand in your relationship with God right now? What are your hopes for your spiritual life in the years ahead?

Chapter 2

1. Chris has begun drinking too much. Do you think drifting from biblical faith tends to lead to drifting from biblical standards of morality—or is it the other way around? Or is there no particular connection between belief and behavior? Give your opinion.

2. Chris loves his grandfather and sees him as a wise older man he can unburden his doubts to. How have your relationships with Christians affected your faith in God for the better or the worse?

3. Do you like to read theology? If so, how have these studies influenced your relationship with God?

4. Gil, Ronald, and Chris debate balance and passion. Do you enjoy discussing controversial issues with others, or are you more likely to avoid a topic that stirs up disagreement? Why?

5. What risks or benefits do you see in people being passionate about what they believe about God?

Chapter 3

1. Gil is making the most of his homebound state by enjoying what he can see from his window. Do you like to take time to be still and simply observe nature and people, or do you feel that you are too busy to do that much? How can taking time to just be still enrich you as a person?

2. Gil tells Chris, "You've got an open door to talk to me anytime. About anything." How good are you at listening in a receptive way to the doubts or worries of others? How could you get better at this?

3. If there was a time when you consciously committed your life to Jesus, describe how it happened.

4. Gil says, "Almost everyone I've led to Christ...thought...that the point of Christianity was 'being good.'" Do you also tend to equate being a Christian with "being good"? If that's not what following Jesus is really about, what *is* it about?

5. Who is Jesus to you?

6. When have you most strongly felt the love of God?

Chapter 4

1. As Chris shovels the snow, Gil's line of questioning reveals his concerns about Chris's reasons for undertaking religious studies. What are the risks of studying God and the Scriptures impersonally, as if they were mere academic subjects?

2. How does studying theology to *know God* differ from studying theology to *know about Him*?

3. Gil says, "An open mind is like an open mouth. It's meant to close on something." Do you agree or disagree, and why?

4. Do you tend to look at truth as absolute or relative? What's your reason for this?

5. Do you agree or disagree with the common idea that all religions are different roads that lead to the same God? How would you defend your view to someone who took the other side?

Chapter 5

1. In his grief over the loss of his wife, Gil finds comfort in reading the Bible. When and how do you read the Bible? What role does it play in your life?

2. Have you ever had an experience similar to Chris's experience of the presence of God on the night of the jam session at age thirteen? If so, tell about it.

3. After the mountaintop experience of feeling the presence of God at Gil's house, Chris descended into the valley when his parents separated. What experiences in your life have shaken your belief in God?

4. What's your attitude toward the Christian church? When have you experienced real Christian community, and when have you experienced fake Christian community?

5. In his sermon to the young people, Gil warned them of the dangers of going along with the crowd. How

has your desire to be liked and accepted by others influenced your religious beliefs or your spiritual practice?

6. What do you think Gil means when he says, "The world says, 'Be true to yourself.' King Jesus says, 'Be true to your future self'"? Give an example from your life of a time when you were faced with that choice.

Chapter 6

1. Gil is reading the church father Augustine. Who are your favorite spiritual writers? How have they influenced you?

2. Gil's breakfast prayer, borrowed from Augustine, says, "We tasted You, and we feel nothing but hunger and thirst for You." How would you describe your hunger for God—are you ravenous or only mildly hungry, or something in between?

3. Do you evangelize? If so, how do you do it?

4. What do you like or not like about evangelism?

5. Are you more like Chris, inclined to see all religions as equal, none superior to the others? Or are you more like Gil, certain that Christianity is in a whole different category from other religions? Explain.

6. Gil says, "Failure to evangelize is almost always a worship problem.... Whenever you are completely taken with something or someone, you can't help but talk about it." If your passion for Jesus were stronger, how might that affect what you say to others about Him and how you say it?

Chapter 7

1. Gil is plainly unhappy about having to live with the effects of his stroke. What is one disappointment God has allowed into your life that you are tempted to be bitter toward Him about?

2. Are there any blots upon the history of Christianity, such as the Crusades, that make it hard for you to be a Christian? Explain.

3. Chris sums up a part of his grandfather's argument when he says, "So you're saying my criticism of the church is Christian criticism." How might your criticism of the church be "Christian criticism"?

4. Does your awareness of your own failings make you less likely to condemn others' failings—or more likely? Why?

5. Gil is hoping his health will improve. Chris is wondering if his faith can come back to life. The chickadee revives after appearing to die. What sin or failure or weakness in your own life would you most like to be healed of if you could?

Chapter 8

1. Katy and her fellow youth group members rebelled against what they had been taught at church by going along with the "different winds" that were blowing in the 1970s. If you had a Christian upbringing, how have you rebelled against it?

2. What's your opinion on whether God approves of homosexuality or not?

3. Do you have a "Chase" in your life? (Or are *you* "Chase"?) If so, how has this affected your attitude toward homosexuality?

4. How would you like to see Christian churches treat homosexuals differently?

5. What kinds of pressures do you think there will be on Christians as society's view of homosexuality changes?

6. Give an example of one time in your life when you became acutely aware of your need to repent—turn from your sin and turn toward Jesus. What brought you to that point?

Chapter 9

1. The phone call from Chris's dad reopens his most painful wound. Describe a time when you found it hard to forgive someone who had hurt you. What did that situation do to your relationship with God?

2. What is it about your relationship with God that you would like others to pray for, just as Gil intercedes in prayer for Chris?

3. Chris heads to a bar, planning to get drunk, when he doesn't want to forgive his dad. For him, drinking has become a form of escape. What form of escape do you tend to go to?

4. What do you believe about hell?

5. Who do you need to forgive right now? Who do you need to seek forgiveness from?

Chapter 10

1. Gil has reached a point where he no longer sees his career as the most important thing in his life. What gives your life significance?

2. It's been a few months since the loss of Frances, and Gil is still deep in mourning. Who are the loved ones you have lost to death? How has their loss changed you?

3. At the cemetery, Gil hopes that a reminder of the brevity of life will move Chris to start living again for King Jesus. Do you feel a sense of urgency about resolving your spiritual questions, or are you content living with the uncertainty? Why?

4. What do you believe happens to people after death?

5. "Tears and laughter today," Gil says. "Only laughter tomorrow." What have been some of the "tears and laughter" in your life lately?

Chapter 11

1. The party Chris has arranged for Gil is a kind of foretaste of heaven. And heaven, of course, is the "laughter tomorrow" Gil had spoken of. Which joys of life seem like foretastes of heaven to you?

2. The group around the piano sings, "Come, and make all things new; build up this ruined earth, restore our faded Paradise, Creation's second birth." What are you looking forward to about heaven?

3. In what ways have your beliefs changed since you started reading this book?

4. What questions or doubts are you still hoping to resolve?

5. What blessing could you share with someone else?

Acknowledgments

It doesn't take a year to write a book; it takes a lifetime. The experiences of our past and the people we've known and loved shape our vision of the world and provide inspiration for writing.

There is a sense in which Gilbert Walker is not make-believe. I've seen glimpses of him in the three men I've been blessed to have as grandfathers: Nevin Wax, Bill Alexander, and Browder Wyatt. I am thankful for the heritage of faith they have passed down to me, and I hope to pass on that legacy to my children.

I must also acknowledge my debt to one of the brilliant apologists of the twentieth century: G. K. Chesterton, who had the unusual gift of turning things upside down so we may at last see them right side up. Chesterton fans will see that I've adapted a number of his memorable aphorisms in this book.

Thanks to Wanda Thurmond and Larry Reed for allowing me to get away to Monterey, Tennessee, and spend time in my great-aunt Mabel's old home—a place where the joy of yesteryear still emanates from every room.

I'm grateful for friends (Greg Breazeale and Zach Kirby), family members (Kevin and Rhonda Wax, Tiffany Mangus, and Justin and Weston Wax), and coworkers (Marty Duren, Micah Carter, and Philip Nation) who gave honest feedback as the manuscript slowly took shape.

Thanks to Andrew Wolgemuth, who saw the potential of this project and helped it develop from start to finish.

Thanks also to Brandon Clements, Dave Kopp, Eric Stanford, and Pamela Shoup, editors whose insights helped me discover the best way to tell this story.

Most of all, I thank my wife, Corina, for believing I could and should attempt to write a fiction book and supporting me during the process.

23   *To be is to be graced.* I first heard this marvelous phrase from James K. A. Smith, who tells me he got it from Augustine.

33   *Thou art my beloved Son.* Mark 1:11.

33   *Sharper than a two-edged sword.* See Hebrews 4:12.

45   *And we of all people.* See 1 Corinthians 15:19.

54   *Thy word is a lamp unto my feet.* Psalm 119:105.

67   *And, when You are poured out on us.* Augustine, *The Confessions of St. Augustine,* no trans. (Nashville: Thomas Nelson, 1999), 3, adapted. Augustine originally wrote his *Confessions* in 397–98.

67   *You were always by me.* Augustine, *Confessions,* 26, adapted.

68   *Satisfied and vanquished* and *pleased and fettered.* Augustine, *Confessions,* 158.

68   *And now You set me face to face.* Augustine, *Confessions,* 162–63, adapted.

69   *Lord, You called and cried out loud.* Augustine, *Confessions,* trans. Henry Chadwick (Oxford: Oxford University Press, 1991), X.xxvii (38).

76   *Go therefore and make disciples of all nations.* Matthew 28:19, ESV.

76   *The world would hate those who follow Him.* See John 15:18–19.

76   *His disciples would be fishers of men.* See Matthew 4:19.

84   *The meek will inherit the earth.* See Matthew 5:5.

95 *The old, old gospel.* Charles Spurgeon, "Sermon for New Year's-Day" (Metropolitan Tabernacle, London, January 1, 1885).

102 *King Jesus is a moral zealot.* Scot McKnight, *One.Life: Jesus Calls, We Follow* (Grand Rapids, MI: Zondervan, 2010), 109.

102 *Every time you or I or anyone else even lusts.* See Matthew 5:28.

103 *Go, and sin no more.* John 8:11.

104 *John the Baptist called out the king.* See Matthew 14:3–4.

106 *Beneath the shadow of the cross.* Augustus Toplady, "Redeemer! Whither Should I Flee," 1759.

106 *Thanks be to God.* See Romans 7:25.

112 *And such were some of you.* 1 Corinthians 6:11.

112 *Saved to sin no more.* William Cowper, "There Is a Fountain Filled with Blood," 1772.

124 *For I will forgive their iniquity.* Jeremiah 31:34.

133 *Rejoice not, that the spirits are subject unto you.* Luke 10:20. This was the response given by Pastor Martyn Lloyd-Jones when asked a similar question at the end of his life.

136 *The last enemy to be destroyed.* 1 Corinthians 15:26, ESV.

137 *In all these things we are more than conquerors.* Romans 8:37–39.

141 *"I've Got a Tiger by the Tail."* Buck Owens, 1964.

141 *"He Stopped Loving Her Today."* Bobby Braddock and Curly Putman, 1980. Originally performed by George Jones.

141 *"The Richest Man (in the World)."* Eddy Arnold, 1955.

142 *Come, for creation groans.* Horatius Bonar, "Come, Lord, and Tarry Not," 1846.

About the Author

Trevin Wax is managing editor of The Gospel Project at Life-Way Christian Resources. His other books include *Holy Subversion: Allegiance to Christ in an Age of Rivals, Counterfeit Gospels: Rediscovering the Good News in a World of False Hope,* and *Gospel-Centered Teaching: Showing Christ in All the Scripture.* He contributes articles to magazines such as *Christianity Today,* speaks regularly at churches and conferences, and writes one of the most popular Christian blogs on the Internet. A former missionary to Romania, Trevin now resides with his wife, Corina, and their children in middle Tennessee.

To find Trevin online, go to:

- The Gospel Project—www.gospelproject.com
- Kingdom People—http://trevinwax.com/
- Twitter—https://twitter.com/trevinwax